I've travelled the world twice over,
Met the famous: saints and sinners,
Poets and artists, kings and queens,
Old stars and hopeful beginners,
I've been where no-one's been before,
Learned secrets from writers and cooks
All with one library ticket
To the wonderful world of books.

© JANICE JAMES.

MOUNTAIN OF FEAR

Panic welled up in her. Was it stalking her in the impenetrable gloom? There was a shriek of a car horn, an angry shout, and she leaped back. What terrifying secret lay in the Cleft of Fenris? What strange gods were worshipped — and were the stories of human sacrifice really true? Beautiful Margaret Buchanan knew that unless she penetrated the mystery that had claimed the lives of her father and her lover, her own soul would be possessed by a force of evil she was powerless to resist.

RONA RANDALL

◆

MOUNTAIN OF FEAR

Complete and Unabridged

ULVERSCROFT
Leicester

First published in Great Britain in 1989 by
Severn House Publishers Limited
London

First Large Print Edition
published September 1995
by arrangement with
Severn House Publishers Limited
Surrey

British Library CIP Data

Randall, Rona
    Mountain of fear.—Large print ed.—
Ulverscroft large print series: mystery
I. Title
823.914 [F]

    ISBN 0–7089–3381–5

Published by
F. A. Thorpe (Publishing) Ltd.
Anstey, Leicestershire
Set by Words & Graphics Ltd.
Anstey, Leicestershire
Printed and bound in Great Britain by
T. J. Press (Padstow) Ltd., Padstow, Cornwall

This book is printed on acid-free paper

1

MARGARET DRUMMOND dropped the reins of her ash-gray mountain pony and slid from the saddle, harness bells jingling as she did so. Her Sherpa porter caught the reins adroitly. The leather strap bearing her load of photographic equipment fitted neatly into a dent across the crown of his head, a dent caused by years of suspended load-carrying. By this method he could transport several hundred-weight, compared with which Margaret's cameras amounted to nothing. Taking long-distance shots of Himalayan peaks required only minimal climbing equipment.

She had come to Nepal on a free-lance job, welcome because it separated her from Edinburgh and a problem she was unsure how to resolve, and now that she was here the terrain fascinated and excited her. It was everything her father had told her to expect.

A person had to see these fantastic

peaks in order to appreciate them; no human mind could conjure up their majesty or imagine that those giant ranges of glistening ice and snow hid the barren black plateau of distant Tibet which, at fifteen thousand feet, was the roof of the world.

Her attention was suddenly attracted by an ancient temple partially hidden by undergrowth. The chance of photographing something unique was too good to miss, but to her astonishment her Sherpa porter backed away.

"Devil's place!" he warned. "No temple now — place of devils!"

His stocky legs, in their Nepalese trousers, shuffled to the other side of the track and despite Margaret's skeptical amusement his tilted eyes begged to be spared.

Her curiosity was heightened by his attitude. Sherpas were stoic and reliable, unafraid of hazards and with implicit faith in their gods, but now the porter made it plain that he preferred to face the wrath of Brahma, Vishnu and Siva combined than the evil which lay within that temple.

"I thought you were Buddhist," she said as she collected her photographic gear, "so why quote the Hindu gods?" Buddhism and Hinduism were the two religions here, often inextricably mixed and sometimes celebrating each other's sacred days.

As she glanced again at the shabby temple roof she thought it must be a long time since anything sacred had been celebrated beneath it, although from where she stood she glimpsed patches which showed that someone had attempted to repair the worst parts. At closer quarters the place didn't appear to be a subject which merited the use of her father's high-powered camera and specialized film. A broken-down, disused temple would be gloomy and uninteresting inside.

A thirty-five millimeter film and a single reflex camera accompanied by flash would suffice, Margaret decided as she pushed her way through a tangle of poinsettia bushes twice as tall as herself, emerging close to the steps of the shabby building.

It was surrounded by a jungle of trees

with massed orchids growing from their trunks, orchids for which her Edinburgh friends would pay a small fortune. She touched a waxen spray, marveling over the size and coloring and texture. She could imagine the rich matrons of Edinburgh's expensive residential areas turning up at the Lord Provost's functions flaunting these costly blooms.

The thought amused her. She wasn't overfond of orchids herself, but as photographic studies these were too good to miss, so she focused her camera, assessing light and shadow, picking unusual angles, lying flat on her back, taking the exotic flowers in close-up and in the mass. Such orchids as these were not likely to come her way again.

It was then that something odd struck her — no paper prayer flags fluttered outside the temple doors. Their absence bore mute testimony to the local attitude. This place, as the Sherpa had warned her, was indeed taboo, but she refused to be discouraged by what she regarded as mere superstition.

She climbed the rickety steps and, as

she expected, the interior was dim, so she clipped the flash-gun into place, focused, shot — and nearly dropped the camera in surprise. The blue flash of light revealed a figure seated within the shadows.

Margaret stammered an apology, adding, "I didn't see you — the place is so dark."

The figure rose and came toward her, and she saw that it was a man wearing a light suit. This was neither a Brahmin priest nor an orange-robed Buddhist. It was a man whose gray hair might once have been dark or fair and whose features were distinctly mid-European.

He said quietly, "I must have startled you. It is I who should apologize."

He spoke English with the precise diction of one to whom it was not a native tongue.

"Am I trespassing?" she asked.

"By no means. Anyone is welcome here. Not that people often come." His smile was wry. "You are the first visitor I have had for a long time."

She shivered slightly, thinking that it must get very cold at this altitude. The man saw the shiver and explained, "The

5

cold is caused mainly by the fierce Tibetan winds whistling over the peaks."

No glimmer of sun penetrated through the slits placed just below roof level to admit air and a certain amount of light. An optimistic architect had designed this place, Margaret thought with wry humor.

"You are right, Mrs. Drummond, but those slits are part of an age-old architectural pattern for temples like this."

She was startled, not only by the use of her name, but because he read her thoughts so accurately. The man smiled and continued, "Windows would tempt the devout to gaze outside instead of concentrating upon their prayers. Not that the devout visit here any more and the only prayers said here are my own."

He placed a threadbare rug upon the floor, apologizing for being unable to offer her anything better to sit on.

"But this is a prayer rug," she said. "Surely it is meant only for kneeling?"

"To a Muslim, yes, but you are a Christian."

"And you don't object to my sitting on it?"

6

"I am not Muslim either, but neither am I Christian, Buddhist or Hindu. My religion is that of the human mind, because only the human mind can transcend body and self — and the sins of either."

She sat down on the rug because she was expected to, but when he remained standing she felt at a disadvantage because it forced her to look up to him.

"How did you know my name?" she asked.

"I projected my thoughts outward, saw you coming, and knew at once who you were."

"You mean you saw me through a window?"

"You have already observed that this temple has none."

She glanced at the door.

"Outside are trees and dense undergrowth," he pointed out. "You had to push your way through to find this place, remember? You couldn't see the entrance until you were almost on top of it."

He moved away into the shadows again, and returned bearing a primitive

7

platter on which were berries and wild fruit.

"I am afraid this is all I have to offer," he said with regret, "and I trust you will not object to sharing the same plate. I possess only one, but in Nepal the practice of sharing a person's plate is as significant as sealing a bond of friendship by the ceremonial mingling of blood, as practiced in ancient Scandinavia."

He set the platter on the rug beside her, then picked up an earthenware lamp and began to replenish it with oil. It reminded Margaret of those used by Romans, centuries ago.

"You are right, Mrs. Drummond. This lamp is Roman, and one of my few possessions. It was given me years ago, when my brother and I were studying archaeology. This lamp was found in Jerash, but I do not keep it for that reason. A man should not have pride in possessions any more than pride in himself or his achievements, only in striving to be a better person. But the lamp is useful. I fuel it with oil, as the Romans did, and it burns for a long time. During the nights when I deny myself sleep it enables me to read."

He indicated some books upon the floor, and Margaret glanced at them with interest. The teachings of Buddha; the Koran; Confucius; Plato's *Republic* — and a Bible.

He sensed her reaction and said, "You are surprised to see a Bible because I am not Christian, and the Koran because I am not Muslim, but they are both wise books and contain much that is good, and all true religions are based on goodness. Truth and goodness are in man himself, the basic qualities of the mind."

The flame from the lamp illumined his face, which was lean and ascetic; his body was also lean, as if food was something rare in his life and of little interest to him anyway. What was he? she wondered. A fanatic, depriving himself for a cause? But what cause could an intelligent man serve by suffering for it in isolation?

In the flickering light from the ancient lamp the place was revealed in all its stark severity. It contained no item for comfort, apart from the threadbare rug and a few primitive utensils. She wondered how he contrived to exist in such a place.

"I get fresh water from a nearby stream," he explained, reading her thoughts once more. "When I need supplies I go down to Katmandu and barter. Not with money, for I live without it, but with orchids — rare orchids which a bounteous nature provides. A hotel in Katmandu gives me food and necessities in exchange for them. They use the orchids for decorating their restaurant tables."

"You have the uncomfortable ability to answer unspoken thoughts." She gave him an uncertain smile and thrust a hand into a pocket of her jacket. "I need a cigarette. You're uncanny."

He held out the primitive lamp and as she stooped over the flame she saw the delicate bones of his hands, and knew they were anything but delicate. There was strength and power in them.

"I think I've heard people talk about you in Katmandu," she said. "Some people call you a guru, but what are you, apart from being a mind-reader?"

"The search for truth brought me to the East some time ago. I studied Yoga and became a guru — a teacher of Yoga — for a time, but that wasn't enough. Having learned how to make my spirit leave my body, I sought greater knowledge and eventually learned how to project my mind into that of another."

"A kindred spirit?"

He nodded gravely.

"And your kindred spirit is — ?"

"My brother. We are twins."

"Now *that* I can understand. It is common knowledge that twins sometimes share thoughts and experiences simultaneously. Psychologists have been interested in it for years. Does your brother live here with you?"

"He is a thousand miles away."

"And you communicate with him across that distance?"

"We communicate with each other," he corrected, unperturbed by her obvious disbelief.

"But this mind-projection works only with him?"

"On the contrary, I can now enter the minds of others, and similarly others can enter mine. Even across a vast space it is possible to know what another mind is

11

thinking and what its owner is doing."

Stunt stuff, that was what Erik would call it. Erik was a practical man, with no time for spiritualism or the occult, or anything of that kind. Erik Sorenson was her real reason for coming to Katmandu, the problem she was unable to solve, and this was illogical, considering she was in love with him.

She became aware that the guru was speaking. " — but you came here to take photographs, Mrs. Drummond. I'm sure you will find the outside more attractive. As you can see, the interior has been virtually stripped."

But she had no desire to go outside yet. This man was interesting, and a welcome change from the gossips at the Royal Hotel in Katmandu.

"Tell me more about this mental telepathy you practice. Isn't it called thought-transference?"

"That is only part of it. Ancient seers knew how to detach the spirit from its bodily imprisonment and set it free. Once that is accomplished, the mind can then go where it wills, and see what it wills . . . "

His voice died abruptly. There was sudden pain in his eyes and tension in his face.

"Are you ill?" Margaret asked swiftly, then fell silent, instinctively aware that his mind had traveled away from her . . .

★ ★ ★

Without warning, the mountain mist dropped like a curtain in front of Angus Buchanan's face, obliterating the fjord far below and the village of Voshanger hugging its shores.

In his hurried descent he had kept the village lights in view because in a world which seemed to have gone insane they represented safety and normality. And now they had vanished, leaving him isolated in a cell of fog with only the jagged buttress, which marked the entrance to the Cleft of Fenris, looming blackly above him.

Mists like this, wraiths which straddled the mountainside without warning, could encircle a man and lead to his death, so he pulled up sharply and stones catapulting from beneath his feet echoed with a threatening sound as they shot into space. One false step, and he would go after them.

The mist spangled his sandy beard and lay clammily upon his rugged face. He passed the back of his free hand across it, the other clutching a camera tightly against him as he debated the choice of remaining where he was until the fog lifted, or of retracing his steps into the higher reaches above where the atmosphere was clear.

But up there lay menace, and he had risked too much already to jeopardize things now. He had to get away, fast.

The thought galvanized him into action and he plunged off to the right, cursing the fog which had obliterated first one landmark and then another which he had noted to guide his return. Now all were gone and he was lost on a stretch of mountainside which the superstitious avoided.

He knew why this place was shunned, for he was as familiar with the myths and legends of this part of western Norway as he was with weird tales of the Himalayas and of wraiths reputed to haunt his native Glencoe, and although he was a man of action, not prone to heed nightmare accounts of phantoms and hauntings, he wouldn't have been surprised if some hideous shape had risen before him. Especially after the horror he had just witnessed.

He pulled himself together. This was not the time to dwell on the past half-hour, up there in the Cavern of Fenris. The scene had outraged his senses and alerted every self-protective instinct. That was why he had to get away before he was discovered and his vital evidence destroyed.

To get that evidence he had risked his life, and he was determined to place neither in jeopardy now. So he went carefully, inching his way forward, regretting the loss of his powerful torch which had rolled away just outside the entrance to the cleft. At that moment he had been intent only on escape, but in his haste he had stumbled and in saving his precious camera the torch had gone crashing down the mountainside. He could have done with its penetrating quartz-iodine beam right now.

But the camera was more important, because its film recorded the proof he had set out to collect, and which he would take back to his laboratory in Edinburgh. Once there, it would be processed in secret.

His feet slithered dangerously on unseen ground, and he forced himself to wait in the hope that the fog would thin out, but every moment was one of tension. He was alone, but not alone. Danger was like a hound baying at his heels.

He took a deep, steadying breath. In the course of his long career as a mountaineer and photographer he had become accustomed to hazards, and although he had never experienced one such as this, he did what he always did at such moments: he felt instinctively for the wallet containing his daughter's photograph, because contact with it meant contact with everything which mattered most in his life. But now shock ran through him. The photograph was missing.

Still clutching his precious camera, he searched frantically through his pockets

16

until forced to accept the truth. He had lost it. It must be lying up there, where he had stumbled in hurried retreat.

His heart contracted, and the lines eched upon his face became anxious. In his mind's eye he could see his daughter's features lying exposed to the sky; Margaret at eighteen, startlingly like her mother — dear, dead Nina who had been taken from him so mysteriously when the child was barely two. He had taken the photograph a couple of years before Margaret's marriage to young Drummond, and captured the gentle innocence of her, an innocence now lost.

But she still had her mother's looks, her smile, her wide-set eyes, and it was these looks which would betray her should the picture fall into certain hands. In that event Margaret would never be safe again.

An additional danger would be the police. If an investigation were carried out later and her photograph found anywhere near the Cleft of Fenris, suspicion would point to her, placing her in greater danger than, unbeknown to her, she was already faced with. The wallet bore his initials and could be traced to himself. He was well known in these parts, although his daughter was not. He had taken good care to keep her away from Norway; he had good reason for wishing her to remain unknown in this country, but if, through association with himself, she should be placed in further danger he would never forgive himself.

There was only one thing to do; get down to Voshanger as quickly as possible, place his photographic evidence in safe keeping, and then go back to find Margaret's picture no matter what the risk to himself. His whole reason for hiding in the Cavern of Fenris had been to save his daughter from disaster, and no careless action of his must be allowed to undermine this intention.

With a swiftness typical of these parts, the mist suddenly rolled away, but the twilight had gone. The blazing sunsets which characterized this part of Norway, and which never ceased to stagger him with their magnificence, had not been manifested tonight. A pall of rain now hung over the distant fjord, dispelling the mist but darkening the waters and the immensity of the surrounding slopes.

Ahead of him a path was discernible in the gloom, and he went forward warily, his thoughts switching back to Margaret. It would be late afternoon now in Nepal's sunlit peaks above Katmandu. She was there with this camera he had perfected, with the newest telescopic lens combined with his latest specialized film, but it wasn't her talent as a photographer which occupied his thoughts now. It was concern, deeper and darker than ever before.

The distance between them was not merely geographic. The rift was greater than that, a gulf which had nothing to do with oceans and continents. Physical nearness was not the same as closeness.

His thoughts snapped with a trigger of alarm; his ears, his eyes, his brain alerted by a whisper of sound. Voices? People? He felt the hair prickle on the back of his neck and stood still, grateful for the oncoming darkness and thankful now that he had not betrayed his whereabouts by torchlight.

He was nearing the bottom of the

slope. If those sounds were indeed voices following him, he could make a dash for it, catapulting down on to the winding road which skirted the foothills and the edge of the fjord. He caught the distant beam of a car's headlights. If he could get down there in time, he could signal for a lift. He estimated that the distance he would have to cover was less than that facing the oncoming car, which would be delayed by the twists and turns of the road. With luck, he would just make it.

The whisper of sound grew louder, but it was not voices. It was wind, a thin high wail, whining from above. He stopped dead, looked backward and upward, and as he did so the wailing ceased.

He knew then that it was no wind. It was like nothing he had ever heard, and its abrupt cessation was eerie. Then suddenly the slopes above were completely blacked out — not by mist, not by rain, not by advancing night, but by a density which descended abruptly, as if a black curtain had been thrown across the scene.

He wanted to move, but was unable to. He wanted to plunge down the last stretch but, mesmerized, remained where he was. Something was happening up there, heralded by a curious noise spinning high in the atmosphere, and it came from the direction of the Cleft of Fenris.

The noise grew in volume. Simultaneously the ridge which concealed the entrance to the cleft was silhouetted against the blackened sky as a bolt of lightning from behind it shot upward like a blazing cannon ball, spun around, and fell. Others followed, until it seemed as if a holocaust raged up there.

The man stared aghast, then plunged swiftly down toward the fjord road and, as he did so, the driver of the approaching car lifted his dark head and stared, fascinated, at the blazing sky.

It was not the first time he had seen an eruption like this. Some of the local inhabitants called it the Rage of Fenris and believed it was the fury of that legendary wolf-god, but others swore it was the Devil's work and when it happened they stayed indoors and prayed, while the bolder ones watched from a safe distance.

As for himself, he had no time for superstition and saw the whole thing as an extraordinary phenomenon of nature. He drove slowly now, watching the cataclysm with a certain awe. Even a man such as he couldn't fail to be impressed when nature went berserk like that.

The Mercedes accelerated as the road reached a downward slope, causing him to brake abruptly as a man staggered out of the foothills, signaling urgently. The headlights spotlighted a sandy beard and a rugged face, features so unmistakable that the driver of the car recognized them at once, and anger blazed in him.

Ramming his foot heavily on the accelerator he shot the car forward, turned the wheel hard left, and swung in a wide arc past the man, leaving him stranded by the roadside.

★ ★ ★

The guru passed a hand across his eyes, shaking his head slightly as if to clear his vision.

Margaret repeated anxiously, "Are you ill?" and the man smiled apologetically, assuring her that he was not, but she had the strange feeling that he had returned to his surroundings almost reluctantly.

Suddenly a touch of amusement flickered about his sensitive mouth and he said, "When you are back at your hotel this evening you will be able to tell friends how you met the mad guru in the evil temple. It will make a good story."

There was no bitterness in the words, but they made her feel oddly ashamed. Already she had visualized some of the reactions — Tony Maitland, from the British Embassy, would be concerned for her, and that garrulous Colonel and his wife from Yorkshire ('Doing the East, my dear, so exciting — but have you *seen* what they do in the streets?') would look aghast and wonder if she had been raped, and unhappy Mrs. Willowby from Chicago, wrapped in riches and an alcoholic haze, would hope she had been.

"Tell me about this temple," Margaret said.

"Originally it was dedicated to the Hindu trilogy, Brahma, Vishnu and Siva, but it was defiled by the cult of Kali, the blood goddess, a legendary figure. Members of the cult gathered here and indulged their wickedness, but although they were destroyed and the effigies of the holy trilogy removed to a more sacred place, Kali's aura remains."

Margaret suppressed a shudder, and the man went on, "A similar cult existed in Norway, the Cult of Fenris the Wolf, and I've heard rumors of its revival. Evil is a powerful influence; even after it seems to have dispersed it can linger, like ripples in a pool until the waters are still. When I ended my Yoga studies with my guru guide, I was alone and decided to remain alone. In solitude I can meditate, project my thoughts to a higher plane, and so combat the forces of evil around me."

"Can you really do this alone?" her tone was doubtful.

"There are others like me, scattered over the face of the earth — people who are dedicated, like myself, to conquering the powers of evil, like witchcraft and black magic, which will lead the world back to the dark ages unless they are fought and overcome." He asked, unexpectedly, "How did you know the temple was here?"

"I didn't — " She broke off. On the upward track she had seen no sign of it.

"I brought you here," he told her gently, "and you were wise to come, despite your Sherpa's warnings. You were intelligent enough to despise his fears, and you are intelligent enough to acquire greater wisdom, if you wish."

"I doubt it," she answered lightly.

"Most people go through life without learning from their mistakes, but not you." He paused, as if weighing his words, then said deliberately, "You won't make a second unhappy choice, but you are on the brink of it. Be wise. Draw back."

Apart from being uncanny, what he was saying was hitting too close for her to want to hear any more. She rarely thought of her impetuous marriage, rushed into when she was twenty, wildly in love and full of idealistic dreams. It was her first real love affair, and should have gone no further than that. A few months would have seen it to its close; she would have suffered disappointment, hurt vanity, but nothing more. A broken marriage left more ragged wounds.

She eyed the figure before her speculatively. Clairvoyance — was that his skill? All this talk about mind-projection sounded impressive, but did it add up? Replace it with terms like clairvoyance or second sight, and an ordinary person could then feel he was facing something familiar, something which went hand-in-hand with fortune-telling, something in which the gullible believed but those with common sense rejected.

But here on a slope of the Himalayas, in a forgotten temple reputedly haunted by evil spirits, with an eccentric guru demonstrating his power of mind-reading, the whole thing took on a sort of macabre significance.

The man said gently, "You have nothing to fear from me, only from others — others whom you trust . . . "

She stubbed out her cigarette. "It is getting late. I must go."

He made no attempt to delay her. As

he helped her to her feet, the touch of his hand was strong. She studied him with interest, wondering if he had cut himself off from the world because he could not fit into the accepted pattern. She felt she should pity him and wondered why she didn't. Instead, she felt that *he* was pitying *her*. There was compassion and concern in his glance; it had been there since the moment when he had broken off in mid-sentence, switching his mind away from her.

As they shook hands in parting, she felt something hard cut into her fingers. It was a ring, large and cumbersome. She gave a start, and he said with concern, "My ring hurt you? I am sorry — "

She looked at it with interest. It bore an image carved from ivory and set in bronze; a strange symbol, reminiscent of the head of a god.

"Varuna, the all-seeing one and the enemy of evil," the man explained. "But you must be familiar with a ring like this."

Margaret shook her head.

"Your father has one, Mrs. Drummond."

"My father? Have you met him?"

"No."

She smiled. "Had you done so, you would know that he never wears rings." She could not resist adding, "Your guesswork was pretty wide of the mark this time."

He wasn't in the least offended. He opened the temple doors and they stepped outside into a world which seemed doubly bright after the temple's gloom. Brilliant butterflies swooped from flower to flower, scarlet poinsettias lifted their bright faces to the sun, and high against the backdrop of a neighboring mountain a giant eagle spread its wings and soared.

She was suddenly anxious to get back to the hotel, take a shower, have a drink.

She said, "I'm sorry for sounding so skeptical, but I do assure you that if my father possessed a ring like that, I would have seen it."

"But you will see it," the man insisted. "Believe me, you will." He took a deep breath and finished, "I have to warn you — you are going to be faced with a crisis for which you will need courage. Great courage."

Her voice shook a little as she asked, "Are you trying to frighten me?"

"No — to help you."

"You'll be saying next that I'm in danger."

She couldn't keep a note of impatience out of her voice, but refused to betray fear, or even to suggest that she took his predictions seriously.

He answered slowly, "Not yet, Mrs. Drummond, but you are going to be. I shall only be able to help you from a distance, but I shall direct my thoughts to that end."

He turned and went back into the temple, leaving her alone and frightened.

2

SHE had left her hired self-drive car at the foot of the mountain track where it joined the rough main road to Katmandu, and as she and her Sherpa covered the rest of the descent she looked about her, awed, as always, by what she saw.

On all sides of the wide valley spread mountain range after mountain range, wave upon wave towering higher and higher until they broke against the sky, and in the distance, veiled by clouds, mighty Annapurna and Everest lay hidden.

The Himalayas, she thought, must surely be the most awe-inspiring sight in the world; she should turn in some magnificent pictures. Her father had told her frankly that he expected her to, which put her on her mettle. She had to justify his confidence in her; she had to merit being entrusted with his latest invention in photographic techniques.

It was because of his laboratory work, in which Angus Buchanan had become increasingly absorbed in recent years, that the Edinburgh financier, Bruce Matheson, had chosen to back him. Matheson's shrewdness, plus his experience in Army Intelligence, enabled him to see the potential in Buchanan's inventiveness, and now Angus was big business in the photographic field.

Margaret possessed her father's tenacity and enthusiasm, but her desire now to prove her talent, and thereby win his praise, was sparked by an equal desire to bridge the ever-widening gulf between them, a gulf which had grown as her affair with Erik Sorenson had grown. Her father's opposition was hardly justified by the excuse that he didn't approve of premarital relationships; she suspected that he wasn't a saint himself, but didn't consider it her concern.

Nor was his position entirely justified by his fear that she might make a second calamitous marriage. She felt there had to be a deeper reason, but what it was he refused to reveal. Consequently, his attitude had sparked a certain antagonism in her, driving a wedge between them.

At the foot of the mountain track she said good-bye to the Sherpa. One more trip — perhaps two, depending on the light — would see the end of her assignment and after that she would leave this remote Himalayan valley and head back to civilized Edinburgh. She wouldn't be sorry, despite the fact that she had reached no decision regarding Erik nor settled in her mind why she was hesitant about marrying again.

This hesitation had nothing to do with her father's attitude. She was blazingly independent, had her own flat in Moray Place and was capable of making her own decisions. She was twenty-five, and the three years since her divorce had done nothing to persuade her to give up her freedom, although Erik was working hard on that.

"I'll want your answer as soon as I return from Norway and you return from the back of beyond," he had insisted, "and there'll be no more of these solitary jaunts for you after we are married. It isn't as if you need to work, and I'm not exactly poor myself. And you must admit, darling, that we're happy together. So why not legalize it?"

What he said was true, and she had no doubt that she loved him. He was thirty, handsome, tall and athletic; a good climber and skier, as was to be expected, being Norwegian, and although domiciled in Scotland since his father had left his post as a lecturer in science at the University of Oslo and taken up a professorship at Edinburgh University, Erik's ties with his native country remained strong. This was mainly due to his wealthy mother, who had a house within convenient reach of Bergen, which she retained mainly for her son so that he could visit his own country whenever he wished.

As he said, he 'wasn't exactly poor,' for besides the house in Norway his mother had a flat in London's Curzon Street which Erik used more than she did. And he was an only child, his doting mother's sole heir. The miracle was that he was unspoiled.

But despite all this, and despite the way they felt about each other, something prevented Margaret from changing their present relationship for the more binding one of marriage. A doubt, an uncertainty, a lack of conviction that it was the best thing to do. A desire to be absolutely *sure* this time.

★ ★ ★

She approached Katmandu on the downhill road from Bodhanath. It was lined with flowering bottle-brush trees, their long scarlet blossoms forming bright curtains of color on either side. Below lay the capital.

It took only a few minutes to drive through the suburbs and, as she entered Katmandu itself, she marveled yet again that in this small town lived a quarter of the valley's population. The unpleasant atmosphere of the place rose up to meet her before she had even passed some of the palaces which tyrannical Ranas had built for themselves during the years of their grip upon Nepal.

To reach her hotel meant plunging first into a labyrinth of filthy alleys, and Margaret thought with longing of the mountain slopes she had left behind.

A dilapidated temple was preferable to squalor such as this, and the temple had been scrupulously clean. The guru could have shown these people how to practice hygiene despite their housing conditions.

If I ever meet him again, she resolved, I'll suggest he applies his mind-projection to these alleys — if all he claimed were true, he should be able to educate the inhabitants by remote control.

Common sense, however, rejected his claims. At the time his predictions had alarmed her, but only because his manner had conveyed an implicit faith in what he saw. It was that which, in a man of high intellect, had made the whole thing impressive and disturbing.

Now she thrust his words to the back of her mind and, minutes later, was out of the slums and in Durbar Square, with its beautifully carved buildings and traditional Nepalese architecture. Then the opulent glory of the Royal Hotel was before her, and she blessed the despotic Rana family for building their innumerable pink palaces and, even more, she blessed the revolution which had overthrown them, opened the closed borders of Nepal to foreigners, and turned opulent Rana dwellings into municipal buildings, or hotels like this one which enabled travelers to enjoy the luxury of an occasional bath, in the event of Katmandu's unreliable electrical supply being available to heat the water.

A few more minutes, she thought with relief, and she would be wallowing in one right up to her chin.

The Royal Hotel was ludicrously magnificent, both in architecture and its grand opera décor; so much larger than life and more unreal than any picture-book illustration of a Sultan's palace, that even Americans made allowances for idiosyncracies like water which ran into the bath when one turned the washbowl taps, and plugs for electric razors which could never be used until nearly midnight because the voltage through the capital dropped almost to zero during the day.

The electricity this evening, Margaret knew by the total absence of lighting, had broken down altogether. Katmandu's electrical supply was on a par with its telephone system, available only at certain hours and not to be relied on even then.

She drove to the front entrance and handed her car-key to one of the Newar porters who sat on the front steps. The man summoned sufficient energy to put her car away and Margaret went on into the hotel.

In the foyer she met Tony Maitland. A nice man, liked by both Westerners and Easterners; a conventional and predictable person who never put out a foot wrong and as a result was an amiable bore. But he was friendly, obliging, and good at his job, part of which was to keep a weather eye open on behalf of Britishers visiting Katmandu, providing those particular citizens warranted more than run-of-the-mill attention. Margaret came in the V.I.P. category because she was the daughter of Angus Buchanan.

She said, "You're early, aren't you? I thought our date was seven-thirty."

"So it is, but the Embassy had a call from your father. He seemed more than anxious to speak to you and will call back around midnight — our time, that is; sixish in Norway. We've arranged with the radio-telephone people for the call to come through as punctually as possible. We've our own lines, as you know, which was why your father called us instead of this hotel — otherwise he might never have got through."

She was surprised to hear that Angus had been trying to get in touch with her. There had been little warmth in their parting, a warning from him about the high mica content of the Nepalese drinking-water and a few other bits of paternal advice and she, in return, thanking him negligently because she was too proud to let him see how much she hated parting from him and how greatly she wanted to bridge the gulf between them

It couldn't have been a more stiff-upper-lip farewell. Nor could it have been more stupid, she thought now, aware of a sudden longing to see him again so that she could lower her guard and try to break down the barrier.

When on a trip, Angus automatically shed the rest of the world; to call her by radio-telephone, and at a time when he must realize she would be out on the job, was surprising, even disturbing. It implied an urgency which caused her a stab of anxiety.

Margaret asked urgently, "Did he leave any message? He's all right, isn't he?"

"Sounded O.K. to me. Just wanted a fatherly chat, I suppose."

She wanted to say: You don't know my father. Paternal chats haven't been his line lately. Warnings and admonishments, yes, but even those stopped when he found I could be as stubborn as he. Suddenly she asked, "Where exactly was he calling from?"

"Bergen."

"But that's not his base. He had gone inland."

"Perhaps he went there on a shopping spree."

She laughed. "Even a visit to his tailor is something to be postponed until all his suits are falling apart."

"Then perhaps weather conditions were unfavorable for photography or climbing, or whatever he has gone to Norway for." Maitland glanced at his watch. "Time for a quick drink before I shunt back to my flat to change, and after all the foot-slogging you've done today, I imagine you could do with one too."

He piloted her towards the bar, installed especially for non-Muslim tourists who 'did' Katmandu in twenty-four hours and spent most of it quenching apparently unquenchable thirsts, at which they were only beaten by high-ranking non-Muslim Nepalese. A babel of English-speaking voices met them at a full spate.

"A very quick one, Tony," Margaret said. "I see that poor woman from Chicago over there — and *she's* seen *us*."

Mrs. Willowby promptly came over, her lonely spaniel-pup's eyes begging for companionship and, as always, compassion prevented Margaret from cold-shouldering her.

"And what have you been photo-graphing today, dear? The Abominable Snowman?" The woman sailed in with her much-used joke — the Yeti was something which intruded into everyone's conversation, unless they were residents and bored by it. Even hotel proprietors, whose trade had trebled as a result of the myth, had now wearied of telling people that the creature was camera-shy.

Margaret said, "If I've taken a shot of him by accident, Mrs. Willowby, I promise to send you a print."

"My, wouldn't that be exciting! It can happen, you know — I mean photographing something which isn't there. People have taken pictures of ghosts that way, did you know?"

"I've heard tell," Margaret acknowledged, accepting with gratitude the Campari-soda Tony brought her.

Mrs. Willowby chattered on. "I was telling Mrs. Drummond how people nowadays can photograph all sorts of things which can't be seen by the human eye. Spirits, ghosts — that sort of thing."

Or gurus, thought Margaret spontaneously, sitting quietly in shadowy temples . . .

"Fake stuff, of course." Tony sat down beside Margaret. "Drink up, and then you can go in search of that bath you hope for."

The American woman exclaimed. "You weren't expecting to get a bath, were you, Mrs. Drummond? Because if you were, you're going to be disappointed. The electricity's — "

" — broken down," Margaret finished for her, nodding towards candles dotted around the bar. They were stuck into saucers, an incongruous note amidst all this operatic splendor.

Tony Maitland reverted to the subject of trick-photography and asked if Margaret's father had ever dabbled in it.

"Not to my knowledge," she told him, "and I can't imagine his doing so."

"I didn't know your father was a photographer too," Mrs. Willowby put in.

"A famous one," Maitland said. "During the war his reconnaissance photographs were tremendously useful to the Allies. He was based in Burma first, then here. It was then that your father came under the spell of the Himalayas, wasn't it, Margaret?"

Margaret put down her glass thoughtfully. She had quite forgotten that her father had been here before she was born, training commando troops in climbing. All she had remembered were mountaineering expeditions in the Himalayas, for which he had been official photographer.

She was deep in speculation when she went upstairs. The guru had denied ever meeting her father, but wasn't it possible that he had done so? It couldn't be ruled out, and would satisfactorily explain what he had said about the ring, although she still could not believe that Angus had ever owned such a thing.

As she undressed, Margaret tried to dismiss the matter and to concentrate only on the evening's party ahead. It was to be at the palace of Jung Krishna, one of the richest Nepalese in Katmandu as well as current Prime Minister, so the party was sure to be lavish. But the prospect didn't take her mind off her father's telephone call; nor did it help her to forget the guru and his alarming predictions.

Even as she plunged under a cold shower she could see the man's compassionate face, and hear the troubled note in his voice as he warned her that she was going to need courage. Great courage.

Could the two things be connected

— her father's urgent desire to speak with her, and the guru's warning?

A shiver of apprehension ran through her. He had also foreseen danger to herself, and despite her determination to forget the whole thing she was suddenly more afraid than when they parted. Fear was an active, vibrant current running through her.

3

AS she expected, the party was lavish and the same faces were there. Embassy officials and their wives, lesser staff members with or without wives, visiting notables, a few wealthy tourists like Mrs. Willowby and the Yorkshire couple who had somehow managed to get invitations, and everyone agog because the King's nephew was expected.

Unfortunately he was late, and because etiquette demanded that no refreshments should be served before the arrival of Royalty everyone was getting very thirsty, particularly Mrs. Willowby who relieved the tedium of waiting by demanding of Margaret, "What's all this I hear about you visiting the mad guru at the forbidden temple?"

Margaret reflected that news traveled fast in Katmandu. One Sherpa porter had only to talk to another.

The Yorkshire woman pricked up her

45

ears. "Is it true? What was he like? And was he embarrassed, having a woman visitor? He's a bit of a hermit, I understand."

Margaret answered coolly, "It wasn't a social call. I thought the temple had photographic interest."

The two women looked disappointed, but at that moment the Prince arrived and all conversation was silenced while a row of Nepalese officers in black and red uniforms took their places at the head of a line to be presented. Next came high-ranking Nepalese officials and their sari-clad wives, followed by foreign diplomats and their families, plus selected guests from the foreign colony.

Margaret, with Tony Maitland, was amongst the British Embassy group, and as they waited to be presented Tony murmured, "We'll get out of this as soon as possible. Everyone will be gossiping about your visit to that lunatic."

She retorted, "He is *not* a lunatic. I prefer his company to this prattling bunch."

The Prince was small, but dignified and courteous. His smile was particularly warm for Margaret, whose father, he said, was greatly admired in Nepal.

"No one has ever photographed our mountains so expertly as he, and now I hear you are following in his footsteps. *Our* women would be too nervous to go up the Himalayan slopes alone, nor," he added with a smile, "would their husbands allow it. I trust we shall have an opportunity to talk again before the evening is over, Mrs. Drummond."

Once the Prince was seated and served, guests were permitted to eat and drink at whatever table they could seize. Somehow Mrs. Willowby found her way into the British Embassy party, and promptly announced that Margaret was going to tell them about her meeting with the guru. Turning to her wide-eyed, she finished, "My dear, weren't you frightened? The things I've heard about that man!"

"Rumors, I'm sure," Margaret replied.

The Colonel's lady cut in. "Is it true that he is psychic and foretells the future? And did he foretell yours?"

Margaret was embarrassed, aware that the conversation was being overheard by the Prince, whose opinion of Europeans would hardly be improved by such gossip.

"He is obviously a madman," the Colonel pronounced heavily.

"You know him, then?"

"We-ell — we haven't exactly met, but I've seen him down here in Katmandu, carrying bouquets of orchids. Like these dropouts who are flocking here, flower people — hippies . . . "

"All hippies aren't dropouts," Margaret pointed out. "Some are living as they believe life should be lived, rejecting materialism. The guru lives the same way, and *he* is good."

Margaret wanted to get up and leave, but courtesy demanded that she should remain until after the departure of the Prince.

Mrs. Willowby suddenly exclaimed, "My, but did you ever see anyone eat so fast as that sample of Nepalese Royalty? All that food gone in no time — and now, would you believe it, he's getting up to go!"

"That is the custom in Nepal," Tony Maitland told her. "Unlike parties at home, one leaves when one has eaten, so one never outstays one's welcome."

Everyone rose as the Prince rose, and all conversation ceased, consequently his words echoed in the silent room as he paused beside Margaret and said, "Please convey my respects to your father, Mrs. Drummond, and tell him how greatly I admire the courage of his daughter in climbing our Himalayan slopes alone."

"It doesn't require courage, Your Highness. With a good Sherpa porter I have nothing to worry about, and the fascination of my job leaves no time for thinking of anything else. Photography is an absorbing business."

"So your father used to tell me. And where is he now — at home in Scotland, or traveling again?"

Margaret admitted that her father was in Norway on what he had said might be a prolonged trip. Angus had indicated that things might delay him, but precisely what things he had declined to say. She had questioned him no further because she was accustomed to his departing on sudden trips and taking as long as he liked over them.

Now she found herself wondering just why this particular trip to Norway, which was only one of many he had made to that country during the past few years, might be particularly prolonged.

She heard the Prince saying, "He has gone to Norway to be amongst the mountains, of course. And perhaps because it is a land where legends and folklore are almost as ancient as here in the East. I remember that stories of our Himalayan gods were always of interest to him. A man of great intellect, your father, but also a man of great wanderlust. Has he passed this wanderlust on to you?"

Margaret was surprised to hear that legends and folklore had appealed to her father, and as for him being interested in stories of ancient gods, that was also surprising — too surprising to be credited in a man so down-to-earth. As for his wanderlust rubbing off onto herself, she wasn't sure. After a trip she was always glad to get home, anxious to put her roots down again. And yet, since the breakup of her marriage, she had felt rootless even in Edinburgh.

She became aware that the slanting

eyes of the Prince were watching her shrewdly. He had the enigmatic quality of the East — the impassive face which appeared to comprehend nothing, but to see everything.

"Perhaps," he said quietly, "you are merely marking time, Mrs. Drummond. But a woman like you should not mark time too long. Travel and adventure are for men, although I know that in the Western world this is not always considered true." His voice returned to normal as he added, "And now I gather you are being questioned about your visit to our guru."

There was embarrassment amongst the surrounding guests and, without glancing at them, the Prince knew it. His slanted eyes twinkled as he continued, "Anyone who does something unusual, particularly a woman, and even more particularly a young and attractive one, becomes a target for comment and speculation. I learned that when I was a student at Oxford. And now I find myself equally curious. What made you go to the temple, Mrs. Drummond?"

"I saw it amongst the trees, Your

Highness, and was drawn to it somehow."

"By the guru, I am sure. And he would have a reason. Not a bad reason, but a good one, because he is good himself."

"I merely wanted to photograph the place."

"I have no doubt he planted that idea in your mind, and behind it he had sound motivation. The man is holy, Mrs. Drummond. He helps people whatever their faith or nationality. He helped me when I was sick and, according to my doctors, with little hope of living. He brought his mind-power to bear on me and said I would recover. And I did."

Margaret was at a loss for an answer. She had decided to ignore everything which the man in the temple had said, but now the words of this Eastern prince seemed to place a disturbing emphasis upon it.

"If our holy man made predictions, Mrs. Drummond, if he warned you in any way, you would be wise to take it seriously. I have never known him to be wrong, and a meeting with him should be remembered — never dismissed."

★ ★ ★

Margaret and Maitland left very soon after the Prince, and as he drove to the British Embassy Tony remarked cheerfully that as a result of the Prince's approval no one would think the worse of her because of her visit to the temple.

"There is no reason why anyone should," she said. "If I had spent the night there, nothing would have happened, if that's what you're implying."

He apologized quickly, and Margaret went on, "All I *do* know is that the man is psychic. He knew my name, without my revealing it. He knew about my father."

"So does everyone around here. You don't need to be psychic to hear about the famous, and the news quickly spread that you were Angus Buchanan's daughter. The man obviously heard of you when he was down in Katmandu."

Margaret shrugged and let it go at that. It still didn't explain the ring, or the guru's statement that her father possessed a similar one. Angus would smile when he heard about that.

As for the warning that she would need courage to face a crisis in her life, everyone needed courage, and and crises occurred in everybody's life, sometimes big, sometimes small. It needed courage to climb a mountain. It needed courage to get through a bad marriage and more courage to contemplate a second, in case that too went wrong.

As for the threat of danger to herself, that was part of life, from crossing the road to boarding hi-jacked airplanes. You took your life in your hands wherever you went and, like her father, she had learned to face up to it — perhaps more than most. Climbing did that for you. As they turned into Lain Chaur, where the Embassy was situated, Margaret's good humor returned and she was able to forget the guru's predictions.

Until later.

The call came through on time, but it was not her father's voice which came intermittently through sputtering static. Margaret listened tensely, waiting for Angus to come to the line, assuming that the sporadic words were merely those of the long-distance operator connecting the person-to-person call.

Suddenly, the interference ceased and the voice came more clearly, speaking English with the careful enunciation of one to whom it was not a native tongue.

"You do not know me, Mrs. Drummond. I am a friend of your father — "

The voice was drowned again and alarm shot through her, deepened by frustration as she listened to the surge and crackle leaping toward her across the world, vibrating through vast emptiness like the forerunner of disaster.

She shivered and her fingers tightened on the receiver. She mustn't let imagination run away with her. She must keep calm. No doubt Angus had merely gone climbing and failed to come back in time.

But that didn't make sense. He had booked the call from Bergen, which meant that he would have made a point of getting back there for it. He wouldn't have gone on a mountain trip in the meantime.

Suddenly she felt more than apprehensive. It was impossible to stand there listening to the surging emptiness, so she called helplessly, "Hello — ? *Hello* — ?" but the words came back at her, hollow and mocking. Then the static ceased and the voice came through again, clearer than before.

"Your father asked me to telephone in his absence. He wanted to break the news himself, but he had to go — "

Margaret demanded urgently, "News? What news? And what do you mean — he had to go? Go where?"

Atmospherics roared again, drowning the distant voice until it was unintelligible. She waited in a fever of impatience, but her agitation had lessened. If her father had had to go somewhere, it meant that he was all right, and wherever he had gone it had obviously been on impulse — probably because the light was suddenly ideal for photography. There was a logical explanation; there had to be. She took a deep, steadying breath and waited for the voice to come back again.

It did so abruptly, loud and clear and shocking.

"It is about Mr. Sorenson . . . "

"*Erik?*"

The voice faded again. It was like listening to the ebb and flow of a tidal wave threatening to drown her.

She had had no idea that her father and Erik were in Norway together. Erik had gone there several days before Angus and was using his mother's house some distance from Voshanger, and the fact that the two men had never been great friends indicated that a meeting between them could only have been accidental.

To calm herself, Margaret insisted in her mind that whatever the news, it could be nothing disastrous. Perhaps only that Erik was returning to Edinburgh earlier than expected and wanted her to go too.

But reason argued that in such an event Erik would have telephoned personally.

Alarm came leaping back. She called helplessly down the line, unable to control her anxiety, and suddenly the interference ceased and the far-away voice said with horrifying clarity, "He is dead, Mrs. Drummond. Mr. Sorenson is dead."

4

THE Boeing from Delhi, which had connected with Margaret's plane from Katmandu, was an hour out of Frankfurt when the radio began to be troublesome, but not until touchdown approached was it announced that an unexpected delay of several hours, as opposed to the usual quick stop, would be necessary.

To some travelers it made a welcome change from the monotony and restrictions of long-distance flying. To others it meant frustration and delay. To Margaret it meant nothing.

She had been sunk in the aftermath of shock throughout the flight, stunned to such a degree that she had given no thought to questions which now began to stir and which had to be thrust down because no answers could be found until she was back in Edinburgh and saw her father again.

A stewardess paused beside her, checking

seat belts. Margaret had made no attempt to fasten hers, so the stewardess did it for her, saying anxiously, "Do have something to eat in Frankfurt, won't you? You've had nothing since coming aboard. The airline bus will take passengers into the city."

Margaret acknowledged the stewardess's advice with a tilt of her mouth which was meant to be a smile. Even that was an effort, for food held no appeal. She had eaten nothing since Tony Maitland had taken charge after the phone call from Bergen.

In a daze, she now recalled him taking the telephone receiver from her numbed hand. After that, he had handled everything with a surprising lack of fuss. She had to get home as quickly as possible, and it was he who arranged it, contacting the airport at Katmandu, checking on the connection at Delhi and making sure that she obtained a reservation.

The jet touched down, powerful brakes screaming to a halt, thrusting her unresistant body hard against the back of her seat. A steward unlocked the doors

59

and the passengers unfastened their seat belts. Automatically, Margaret did the same. She had no desire to leave the plane, and the stewardess knew it. She watched Margaret drag herself to her feet and follow the others, fatigue in every line of her. Throughout the flight she had been slumped in her seat, wanting nothing more than a hot drink and a tranquillizer during the long night. Even then, she had scarcely slept. There was a quality of stoicism about her, the stewardess thought, a tenacity — something which refused to allow her to crack.

Margaret's one thought now was to telephone her father. She knew Frankfurt fairly well and once through the airport formalities she took a taxi straight to the Frankfurterhof Hotel.

The day was murky, and Frankfurt's granite face more gray than ever. Even the hotel's small garden was cheerless, and after paying off the taxi she walked along the path which led straight from the sidewalk, eager to escape from the damp depression of dripping trees and gathering fog.

The hotel's Victorian façade looked up eerily, its solid splendor dimmed by the day's dreariness. Garden tables stood deserted, with chairs propped against them, and trees sighed heavily. Not even the blaze of light from within the building dispelled a sense of impending gloom.

She pushed open the heavy doors, welcoming the brilliance after the murk outside. The hotel was large, luxurious, and dignified, run with impersonal German efficiency, the long mahogany reception counter at the far end of the foyer manned by impeccably groomed gentlemen wearing impeccable suits and speaking English with almost impeccable accents. All this should have been reassuring. It was not. The air of cold efficiency was chilling, and increased her longing for home.

Tony Maitland had cabled her father the number of her flight to London, also of her local flight from there to Edinburgh, and although the delay in arriving at London would be announced at Heathrow, this would not affect domestic air routes. Therefore Angus would have no way of knowing that she had missed the Edinburgh flight.

She might miss not one, but several, and she had no desire for her father to kick his heels waiting. She sought these excuses to convince herself that the call was essential, although she knew it was not. Angus was too seasoned a traveler to depart for any airport without checking a plane's progress before-hand, and he would waste no time in merely checking the one to Edinburgh. He would find out himself whether or not the aircraft from Delhi was delayed.

The truth was that she wanted to hear his voice. She was reaching out to him now across the rift which he had tried to bridge and which she had maintained by clinging steadfastly to Erik. She was taking the first step in rehabilitating herself after shock, reaching out for a contact with home and with the one person who represented it most.

She was so intent upon getting to a telephone that she paid no attention to her surroundings, or to a man leaning against the reception desk. She was vaguely aware that the adjoining clerk was talking to someone, but that was all. The powerfully built man beside her made no impression, and she failed to notice his scrutiny as she booked a call to the Voshanger Hotel in Voshanger, Norway, the number of which she did not know.

She felt apprehensive as she waited, although she knew nothing could go wrong. Soon she would hear Angus's Scottish voice echoing down the line, assuring her that he would be home before her and waiting to meet her at the airport. She needed this reassurance badly, for beneath her tension lay a feeling of threat which she attributed to the pervading gloom outside. A drink was what she needed, perhaps; a brandy to steady her. She was letting shattered nerves take control.

The desk clerk, coldly efficient, told her that he would trace the number and let her know when the call came through. Margaret turned away, and as she did so she saw a dark-browed face looking down at her, and the feeling that it had been watching for some time became a sudden and sharp conviction.

She felt annoyed. Hotel lounges were notorious places for pick-ups and to make it plain to this man that his attention was unwanted she sat down in a chair some distance away, her back turned, fumbling in her bag for cigarettes and lighting one automatically, at the same time telling herself not to. Smoking was a habit she had given up. The cigarette in the temple had been her first for a long time, but now shredded nerves were creating the need again. It had to stop, she reminded herself, but continued to draw on the cigarette as she waited impatiently for her call.

The man walked by, looking at her out of the corner of his eye. Her annoyance increased. She stared straight ahead, ignoring him, then heels clicked beside her and the reception clerk gave a precise bow.

He regretted that her call to Norway would be delayed; the hotel's lines were overloaded with long-distance calls; a jet to London had been held up and many passengers had come here to telephone.

Disappointment, coupled with vexation, was sharp. She should have anticipated that other passengers would have the same idea and that she would inevitably be one of a queue. She stubbed out her cigarette in frustration and asked just how long she would have to wait.

"It is impossible to say, Madam. It depends on how quickly the lines clear, and that depends on how long other calls take, but I should think perhaps an hour."

Behind glinting spectacles she saw the receptionist's cold eyes taking in every detail of her appearance, and although they seemed to register approval she felt chilled by the man. Simultaneously she was aware of the dark stranger watching and listening nearby, and a feeling of desperation rose in her. She had to get away from this place.

"Cancel the call," she said abruptly, and gathered up her belongings. She had forgotten to refasten her bag after taking out the cigarettes and now some of its contents spilled onto the armchair, including her air ticket and reboarding card. She pushed them back hurriedly and headed for the door, quickening her steps as she reached the garden. They echoed with a curiously muffled sound as she hurried along the path.

She was surprised to find that the fog had thickened considerably.

Beyond dismal trees, the eternal clang of Frankfurt's streetcars vibrated eerily. She could see them moving like lumbering beasts shrouded in draperies of fog. She had never heard this noisy city so muffled, never before felt it to be sinister, but she did now. By the time she reached the sidewalk the solid front of the hotel had almost disappeared behind her.

She looked back, undecided as to what to do or where to go, feeling light-headed with fatigue and strain, and at that moment a swirl of mist blotted out the last glimmer of light from the hotel windows, leaving her marooned in an island of fog.

Panic welled up in her. She felt cut off, alone, stranded in a sightless world. At the same time she felt vulnerable, the target for attack, completely defenseless. Any sinister shape could loom up, strike, and disappear; a cry for help would be stifled by the blanket about her. Suddenly the guru's prediction of danger shrieked in her memory.

Was it coming? Was it here, waiting for

her, stalking her, crouching out of sight, creeping up ready to spring, whispering its threat in the impenetrable gloom?

She fought against increasing terror and took a blind step forward, straining her eyes for a glimpse of the pavement, not knowing whether to grope her way to left or to right. But the blind step landed her straight into the path of looming fog lamps. There was a shriek of a car horn, the angry shout of a voice, and she leaped back into a smothering cocoon of fog which wrapped around her, cold and damp and penetrating.

She forced herself to take a steadying breath, realizing now that she had been foolish to leave the safety of the airport and head, alone, for this alien, fog-bound city. What impulse had prompted her? What twist of fate had set her down here, and for what reason? To fulfill the prediction of danger made by the man in the temple?

She thrust the thought aside. She had set out to telephone her father, and that resolve she would carry out. She had to find some quiet place, a small hotel or restaurant which was not busy. She took a hesitant step forward and at that precise instant a break in the fog revealed the hotel path and the looming figure of a man.

She recognized him at once, and her heart contracted in alarm. Simultaneously, he saw her and quickened his stride. She took a turn to the right and stumbled forward, her heels sending out staccato sounds which he would surely hear. She flung a desperate glance over her shoulder, but could see nothing; the curtain of fog had mercifully descended again. But she could hear heavy footsteps following relentlessly, and knew they were his.

5

FEAR spurred her forward. She stumbled blindly into passers-by. Someone grabbed her arm, protesting volubly in German, and immediately the pursuing footsteps increased.

Margaret wrenched free, intent only on escaping from her unknown pursuer; there was menace in his determined tread. She groped before her unseeingly, then, on her right, she heard the muffled rumble of traffic, indicating that the road lay in that direction and that if she veered to the left she might reach the walls of buildings. She moved sideways, arm out-thrust, and met the reassuring solidity of brick.

She moved quietly then, guiding herself along the wall, pausing between steps to listen intently. The man was still following. His tread had slowed, but remained relentless.

Suddenly Margaret's groping hand fell

into space. The wall had finished, but her foot touched something hard. She realized that it was a doorstep, and that the space was a recessed doorway standing flush with the pavement. She stepped inside and waited. Since she had been unable to see this entrance, other people were also unlikely to see it. She was safely hidden.

Scarcely breathing, she listened again. The man's footsteps were now close, and although muffled they sounded loud in her ears. A moment later he was almost on top of her and she drew back, pressing hard against the door behind her and standing rigid as the footsteps walked by. She saw the man's solid bulk pass like a shadow.

She remained rigid until the shadow had gone, then she leaned limply against the door.

Seconds later, her brain took control again and she knew that she had to retrace her steps, grope her way back to the Frankfurterhof, and have the good sense to make the call from there. By now the long-distance lines should be in less demand and the wait considerably shortened.

She stepped out of the porch and guided herself by the wall again, but in the reverse direction. Her tension had lessened to such a degree that she was able to reason calmly.

And reason told her that if she returned to the Frankfurterhof, the man was likely to do the same. By now he would have lost all sound of her step so he would give up and go back, which meant that this was the last thing she herself must do.

She leaned against the wall, trying to think sanely. Picking up a taxi would be hopeless in this fog. She was totally lost, and a feeling of panic returned to her. Simultaneously, the words of the man in the temple returned to her also.

Damn that guru, with his thought-reading and predictions! It was ridiculous to think of them now; anyone lost in a fog, alone in an alien city, needed courage; it was a situation in which anyone could land.

She reminded herself that he had been wrong about one thing — the ring which he declared her father possessed and which she knew did not exist. That proved the man was not infallible, and the thought steadied her a little. The very idea of Angus wearing a barbaric ring was ridiculous, so ridiculous that she wanted to laugh. She could feel hysteria rising up in her. Another minute, and she would be standing here in the fog, laughing aloud.

Oh God, help me . . . I'm alone . . . help me!

As if in answer to her panic-stricken prayer she saw the blurred outlines of a neon sign. It was only a few yards distant and she must have walked right past it because it was high above her head. She groped her way back and suddenly its outlines were no longer blurred. They spelled out the words SCHILLER HOTEL.

The neon sign hung above a door so solid that it seemed to shut out the world, and small windows situated high in the brick wall were heavily curtained. For this reason Margaret had walked right beneath them, had she looked up, she would have seen a chink of light between the curtains. Now that chink of light encouraged her to grope for the door handle, which proved to be a large iron ring so heavy that she could only partially turn it.

She slid her hand upward until it touched an iron knocker. The sound of it reverberated in the hall beyond, heavy and somber, and while she waited for an answer she heard the muffled tread of returning footsteps along the street. Out of all the steps intermittently passing, Margaret recognized these at once. The dark man who had followed her was now heading back to the Frankfurterhof and coming this way.

At that moment the door of the Schiller Hotel opened and light fell full upon her. She stepped inside swiftly, scarcely heeding the guttural flow of German from the elderly porter, who seemed to be apologizing for the closed door and explaining that it was necessary on such a night. He slammed it behind him and it echoed with a hollow thud throughout the length of a gloomy passage.

At the far end was a reception desk and behind it sat a fat, sullen woman who gave Margaret no welcoming smile but pointed wordlessly to an open door leading into a small and dimly-lit restaurant. At any other time the place might have appeared quite respectable, but now it seemed sleazy and faintly sinister. The woman's expression, coupled with the shuffling steps of the porter as he vanished behind the scenes, added to a general feeling of unease.

When Margaret indicated by sign language that she merely wanted to telephone, the woman's expression became a glower which deepened even further when realizing that Margaret spoke no German. With a screech the woman yelled "Franz! Franz!" then uttered a string of German oaths when the porter failed to appear. With a despairing shrug she heaved herself from behind her desk and lumbered away into the back of the hotel.

Margaret waited tensely. She could hear desultory conversation from the restaurant and glimpsed an untidy waiter wearing a soiled apron standing in a bored attitude just inside the door. His glance ran up and down her appraisingly. The restaurant seemed half empty, and she wasn't surprised. She could imagine no one wanting to dine in an atmosphere like this — depressing, gloomy, and cold. She shivered, anxious to escape.

It seemed a long time before the grumbling proprietress and the apologetic porter reappeared, although it was little more than a minute. The man spoke some English, and seemed startled when Margaret announced that she wanted to put a call through to Norway, urgently.

Norway? No one had ever made such a request before, not at the Schiller Hotel. In a spate of German he repeated it to the manageress, now squatting like a great fat toad behind her desk. Her eyes bulged in surprise and she promptly launched into a stream of guttural protests which the porter haltingly translated. Local calls were easy; international calls were not. The hotel only had one line. There were other excuses, but they all added up to the fact that making an international call would be a nuisance.

The excuses continued until Margaret opened her handbag and slapped down a bundle of notes more than sufficient to cover the cost and the trouble.

It worked like a charm, and she blessed her foresight in obtaining German marks before leaving the airport. The fat hand swallowed up the money and the sullen face almost smiled. Then the woman pushed a note pad forward and Margaret wrote down the name of the Voshanger Hotel, its location, and added the word *taxi*.

The woman nodded toward a phone booth situated in a corner off the hall. It was in darkness and the light failed to work, but Margaret waited with the door ajar, listening to the strident female voice bullying the telephone operator then hustling the porter to fetch a taxi while the call was put through. In a matter of minutes the telephone inside the booth rang imperatively; Margaret let the door slam and snatched up the receiver.

As she did so, the hotel's front door opened and heavy footsteps walked along the gloomy hall, but the only thing Margaret heard was a distant male voice briskly announcing the Voshanger Hotel.

When she asked for her father there

was a brief and expressive silence and Margaret knew intuitively that Angus had gone, that he had already left for Edinburgh, and that the hotel clerk was about to tell her so, but instead he replied, "Mr. Angus Buchanan? I'm afraid he is not here."

"You mean he has left?"

"No, Madam. He is not staying at the hotel."

"But — he was, quite recently — "

"I'm afraid not, Madam."

Margaret stammered incoherently, "There must be some mistake!"

"No, Madam. The last time Mr. Buchanan stayed here was about two months ago."

She remembered that. A sudden visit. He paid many sudden visits to Norway, always staying at the Voshanger, but she never heeded them. He liked the country and it offered good climbing. These were good enough reasons for him to go there without giving any explanation to his daughter.

"Are you *sure*?" she asked helplessly.

"Quite sure, Madam."

She replaced the receiver, her hand

trembling so violently that she missed the hook at the first attempt. Something was wrong — radically wrong. There was nowhere to stay in Voshanger other than the hotel.

6

MARGARET leaned against the wall of the telephone booth, insisting to herself that the clerk at Voshanger had made a mistake. She would arrive back in Edinburgh to see her father waiting for her at the airport, solid and reassuring, and the sooner she got out of this depressing little hotel and on her way, the better.

The thought of Edinburgh brought Bruce Matheson to mind. He was her father's partner and Angus would have rung him from Norway; they always kept in touch regarding business affairs so if she telephoned Bruce he would surely have news, but that meant he would also have heard of Erik's death and would be commiserating and sympathetic. She couldn't face that. She couldn't talk about Erik to anyone yet.

She dragged herself erect, put a hand against the door to push it open, and from the darkness of the booth looked into the dimly-lit hall and straight at a craggy profile, a dark head, a strong and formidable figure.

Fear took hold of her. He was inescapable, this relentless and sinister man.

She drew back into the shadows of the darkened booth, aware that he must have traced her by something more than guesswork. She remembered the approaching footsteps as she wielded the heavy door-knocker, and the sudden beam of light from within which, gloomy as it now seemed, had spotlighted her. Even through the fog her figure must have been discernible.

From her hiding place she looked at the man's profile. It seemed implacable and determined as he stood there with ill-concealed impatience. The fat woman was not behind her desk and Margaret guessed that the man was impatient because he wanted attention.

She saw him cross to the restaurant, and at that precise moment the door of the telephone booth opened and the elderly porter announced that her taxi was waiting. Margaret snatched up her bag, thrust a note into his hand, and headed fast for the front door. As she passed the entrance to the restaurant she saw the dark man standing with his back to her, questioning the waiter who looked directly at her and promptly nodded in her direction.

The man spun around and for one paralyzed second Margaret looked straight into his eyes, then she was hurrying down the hall and out to the waiting taxi. As she slammed the door of the vehicle she heard a shout from the hotel and caught a brief glimpse of the man's tall figure silhouetted within the entrance, as her own had been.

She drew back sharply, her heart thudding, and as the taxi moved forward she gasped, "Airport — quickly!" but the driver shook his head in protest, indicated the fog, and slowed to a halt after a few yards.

With shaking hands Margaret opened her bag to take out the necessary bribe, aware of the calculating and watchful eyes of the man at the wheel.

She drew out her compact, air ticket, reboarding card, and finally the wallet itself — but something was missing, and with a sickening jolt she realized that it was her passport.

She tumbled the remaining contents of her bag into her lap while the taxi-driver looked on, his eyes focusing with satisfaction on the thick wallet. Here was a fare worth picking up, however bad the weather. He told her, in halting English, that he would take her to the airport, adding that she need not worry — in fog such as this her flight would not leave.

Then he saw her stricken face, and immediately asked what was wrong.

Margaret scarcely heard him, for she was frantically searching her memory for some clue as to where she could have lost her passport, but all she could think was that somewhere between the Frankfurterhof and the Schiller it must be lying on some fog-enshrouded pavement.

She clearly remembered seeing it in her bag when she took out her cigarettes in the first hotel, but what about that gloomy little place she had just left? She tried to recall whether she had seen it when taking out the wad of notes to soften the unwilling proprietress, but could not remember. The man's pursuit of her in the fog had reduced her to a state of helpless confusion.

Now she was numbed by shock. She had never realized before what it actually felt like to be in a foreign country without a passport. Stateless. Homeless. Lost. She passed a shaking hand across her face, trying to conquer panic. The British Consulate; she would contact the British Consulate —

But would it be open at this hour?

The taxi-driver was saying, "You lose something, yes? I take you back to the Schiller?"

She nodded helplessly. The search would have to be made — first the Schiller and then the Frankfurterhof. She thought of the stiff receptionist and his cold, bespectacled eyes with their frank appreciation of her looks, and of the man with the hard features who had determinedly tracked her down. Of the two, the first could be appealed to for help regarding accommodation, but the second . . .

He was the last man she ever wished to see again.

The taxi reversed and stopped beneath the neon sign. The hotel door was closed again, and Margaret braced herself as she walked across to it.

As she did so, a figure loomed out of the fog and seized her arm.

She stifled a scream, and a man's voice said, "Are you looking for this, Mrs. Drummond?"

★ ★ ★

Bruce Matheson shifted his lean frame uneasily in one of the deep leather armchairs of Edinburgh's exclusive Military Club. Outside, traffic roared along George Street, but he was unaware of it; unaware also of the hum of voices in the club bar. His attention was concentrated on the front page of the *Scottish Evening News*, featuring the story of Erik Sorenson's death.

The report added nothing to the facts which Angus Buchanan had briefly told him over the phone. Angus had called him from Voshanger, explaining that his return might be delayed while inquiries were made, but that he would get back as soon as possible, for Margaret's sake.

The newspaper devoted a whole column to the disaster. Sorenson had been killed when climbing somewhere in western Norway. Those peaks could be treacherous, and in some parts glaciers were ever-present dangers, such as the Jostedal which overhung the fjord village of Fjaerland at one point — but that was a long way from Voshanger.

As Matheson sipped his whisky his thoughts flew to Margaret. His concern was for her, more than for Sorenson. He wondered how she had taken the news. Her father must have reached her by telephone, and a grim sort of shock it must have been.

He knew that to get home she would have to travel via Delhi — but first she had to get to Delhi from Katmandu, and Matheson was unsure how long that took. He had contacted all airlines touching down at Delhi to check Margaret's flight number and arrival time, but being a last-minute passenger no booking had yet been reported. He would keep at it, knowing she would come straight home because she could do no good by going to Norway.

Bruce couldn't get Margaret off his mind. He was pretty sure that Sorenson had been in love with her and wanted to marry her, but she had seemed content with their relationship as it stood, a relationship lacking security and permanency. This implied that she was not so deeply in love with Sorenson as he with her, and the thought gave Bruce a feeling of satisfaction. She was the only woman who had seriously attracted him since Paula's death.

His hand went up automatically to the scar on his right cheek. The aircrash had happened ten years ago, killing his wife and young son. He had escaped unmarked, but for this facial wound.

He had tried to achieve forgetfulness in the usual ways — hard playing, hard work. The hard work had at least piled up money. It had become a challenge, then an obsession, and backing Angus Buchanan had brought Margaret into his life. In her Bruce saw the hope of some peace of mind again, companionship, love.

He had thought she would be easy to get, because at that time she was recovering from a broken marriage which, he felt, would make her more responsive to a man of his age. He had the complacency which sometimes accompanies success, and for this reason Erik Sorenson's swift possession of her was a shock. He resented it.

Sorenson's social assets were a further irritation. The man was well-known in Edinburgh society, his parents prominent in the city — his father because of his academic position and his mother because of her wealth. Coupled with good looks and athletic prowess, plus a monied background, Sorenson was one of Edinburgh's most eligible bachelors, but Bruce knew that he had more to offer Margaret than Sorenson had.

Apart from his business tie-up with Angus Buchanan, he had other interests in Bergen and Oslo and Stavanger, and when visiting the Norwegian offices he made a point of getting in some climbing and skiing. He was forty and as lithe as a man of twenty.

Perhaps Margaret would turn to him

now that Sorenson, poor devil, was out of the way. 'Poor devil' could apply to anyone killed in an accident. You thought it when you read of some unknown person's death, turned the page, and went on reading.

Bruce was now ready to turn the page and go on living, and that meant starting with the Midsummer Ball in Edinburgh Castle tonight. He was going reluctantly, because he would have preferred to take Margaret, but it was one of those affairs which amounted to an obligation, one of the highlights of the Edinburgh social scene and invariably patronized by a member of the Royal Family. Successful businessmen were those seen by the right people, with the right people, in the right places, at the right time. Next year, if he had his way, it would be with the right wife. The coast was clear. He would move in and take possession.

He glanced at his watch, aware that he should be leaving. He had already been home and changed, and now the mirrored wall opposite threw back his reflection, handsome in Highland evening dress, the Matheson tartan striking and colorful. Even the scar on his face didn't detract. Some women insisted that it added a touch of distinction and a definite appeal.

He finished his drink and rose. The white-coated barman called a respectful good-night. Matheson still retained his Army rank, having belonged to a famous Scots regiment which had been axed years back and in which he had distinguished himself, as had his father and grandfather before him. After the break he had moved into Army Intelligence, based in Singapore, but after the loss of his wife and son he had broken finally with a military career and launched into the business world, accepting a directorship with a well-known Edinburgh firm holding widespread engineering interests in the United States and Scandinavia, as well as in Britain.

It wasn't long before he had other irons in the fire, private irons of his own. Angus Buchanan was one of them. All in all, he had done well for himself, and was now a prominent tycoon with a house in Edinburgh's Heriot Row, a flat in London's Mayfair, and a home in

Argyllshire which he had inherited from his wife, along with her money.

He was realistic enough to know that the deference shown to him in this club was due to his wealth and his birth rather than to any personal liking. It was the same socially. He moved in an exclusive and snobbish circle, a circle which Margaret criticized — she was a typical product of her generation. Like her father, she was a bit of a rebel. Angus didn't care what a man's background was like, or from where he came, so long as he shared his passionate love of mountains.

"There's no room for social distinction up there on the rock face," Angus would say. "When men are up against the forces of nature there's no difference between them. *You* ought to know that, Matheson. Soldiers are killed on the battlefield in the same bloody way whatever their birth."

But at least, in the Army, there was rank, and this was remembered and observed in this club. The ex-Army batmen and sergeants who staffed the place were still conscious of rank, and when Margaret became his wife she would learn to be proud of her husband's and outgrow this tendency of her father to accept people whatever or whoever they were.

The porter hurried to open the door for him, and then to do the same at his drop-head Rolls parked by a deserted meter in the center of the street. Bruce Matheson followed leisurely, but as he descended the short front steps he paused in surprise. Hurrying up them was his manservant, Wallace.

Bruce frowned. Only something serious could bring the man to the club.

Then he saw concern in Wallace's face and heard it in his voice as the man blurted, "Sorry, sir, but its urgent . . . "

★ ★ ★

As the R.A.C. Jet One-Eleven approached Edinburgh, Margaret began to relax. She even found it possible to look back on the incident in Frankfurt with a certain amount of reason. In retrospect her alarm, and the way in which she had seized her passport with no more than a stammered word of thanks before hurrying back into the taxi and slamming the door, seemed perhaps unnecessary, but the way in which the man had suddenly risen out of the fog and taken hold of her arm had been a culminating shock after his pursuit of her.

Not until her taxi reached the Autobahn, one of a stream of crawling fog-lights, had Margaret's shock begun to recede, instantly giving way to alarming tales of stolen passports and the criminal motives behind such thefts. Then reason argued that the man had had no time to do anything with hers except scan the personal details and learn her name. Reason also pointed out that he could have followed her solely to return it and that her fear had been unwarranted.

But all that was behind her now. Soon she would see her father's powerful figure in the arrival hall, and would want to fling herself on him — but, instead, she would be as undemonstrative as he. Even so, he would know that beneath her self-control she was weeping for her dead lover and would want to do all in his power to comfort her, letting her know without words that if she wanted a shoulder to weep on, he had two and both were hers.

But when she crossed the tarmac and entered the airport building there was no sign of Angus. Instead, Bruce Matheson came toward her. She stood quite still, staring, as disappointment changed to alarm. She knew at once that something was wrong.

When Bruce reached her she jerked, "*Father — where's Father?*"

7

SHE wakened with Bruce's words echoing in her mind. "*He has been killed. In Norway. An accident of some kind . . .* " He had groped for words to soften the blow, but they could only be blunt and truthful.

Margaret sat up slowly. In the dressing table mirror opposite she saw her reflection, shadowed and hollowed with weariness. The features seemed scarcely to be her own; the skin looked taut, as if she had suddenly grown older, or been ill.

She turned away from her image, seeing in it her father's high cheekbones and wide brow, unable to face this reminder of him. The nightmare which had disturbed her sleep became a blinding truth and she closed her eyes, seeking behind them some screen of oblivion, only to discover that such evasion proved to be no refuge at all, for the double tragedy of death was stark and inescapable.

She opened her eyes again and looked

straight into Erik's. His photograph stood beside her bed. She had taken it herself, insisting that he look directly into the camera so that wherever she walked about her room she could turn and meet his eyes.

She met them now. They held that compelling glance which had arrested her the first time they met. He was one of those rare people who could maintain an almost unflinching gaze without in any way making one feel uncomfortable. He had focused it on her that night at the Secretary of State's Reception in the Great Hall of the castle.

That meeting had been momentous, and she remembered now how unwillingly she had gone to what promised to be yet another boring party. Bruce had insisted on taking her; he was being very solicitous at that time, metaphorically taking her by the hand to help her over a bad patch in her life.

This particular affair had proved to be no different from the rest; the same faces, the same voices, the same commiserations about the breakup of her marriage — or the same scrupulous avoidance of any reference to it; the same polite and meaningless conversation with polite and meaningless people, until gradually you had to shout above the din, and your feet ached from standing and your face from perpetually smiling.

And just when she was wondering how to escape, she had looked across the sixteenth-century hall and through a gap in the crowd had seen this man looking at her. He had continued to stare unabashed and she had been almost mesmerized until the gap closed and he disappeared from view.

Then, suddenly, he reappeared, right beside her.

"I'm Erik Sorenson. Shall we escape to the Palace Yard and get to know each other?"

They had done so at once. In the centuries-old court-yard the kilted Pipers who heralded the arrival of guests had folded their pipes and gone. She and Erik were alone.

She could see him now, with the light from the high castle windows shining down on his blond Scandinavian head, and that compelling glance possessing her instantly. He had a magnetic quality and an air of command. When she told him her name he merely replied that he knew it already. "I made up my mind to find out all about you the first moment I saw you."

After that, the rest was inevitable. With him she found the comfort and assurance she needed. He possessed her completely as, he told her later, he had intended to from the first.

That compelling quality was in his photograph, so strong that it was impossible to imagine it being extinguished. But it had been. Climbing, Bruce had told her; exactly how, he had no idea. All he had to go on was the small amount of press information and the brief fact given to him over the telephone by Angus. An accident, her father had said; that was all there had been time to say.

And then Angus had gone out and met with an accident himself.

Two accidents on the rock face. Two expert climbers, and within a day or two both were killed. It didn't seem possible. It didn't make sense. The Norwegian winter with its mountaineering hazards

97

was a long way off. This was a safe time of the year for climbing, but how else could either have been killed?

She had a sudden picture of Erik's athletic body falling . . . falling . . . disappearing into some impenetrable crevasse where he now lay entombed forever. Desolation swept over her as she thought of him lying close to her in the long stretches of the night and realized that they would share no more the quick intimacy which comes with darkness.

With a gesture of pain she turned his picture face downward on the bedside table and immediately looked across the room at the double-framed photographs of her parents. Nina, who had never had a chance to grow old, and Angus in later years, his sandy beard out-thrust, his eyes piercing and intelligent and kind. Life had burned in his eyes as strongly as it had burned in Erik's but, she now realized, in an entirely different way.

She had never compared them before; she tried to do so now. The intensity in Erik's eyes conflicted with the warm vitality of her father's, but the quality of that conflict Margaret could not analyze because grief made it impossible.

It was a shock to realize that, for the first time in her life, she was completely alone. No one could help her over this double grief; she had to endure it silently and get on with the business of living whether she liked it or not, whether it hurt or not.

That was what her father would have said, was saying to her now across the span of their life together; across kindnesses and misunderstandings, closeness and separation; letting her know that despite being two separate and individual people they belonged together.

Angus had always made that clear, without words, without analysis of the special relationship which exists between a father and his motherless daughter, a relationship which could be closer than average. Even so, their lives had been their own and that was how they had lived them, each going their separate ways but always in touch, so that she knew that when away, as he frequently was, he never forgot her and would always come back.

But not this time. From this trip he would never come back, and the rift between them would never be healed.

Unshed tears ached behind her eyes. She had to accept the fact that her father now lay dead in Norway, a country he had visited more than any other and to which he had never once suggested she should accompany him.

The realization struck her suddenly; so did the strangeness of it. It had never occurred to her before because her own life had been too full, packed with the social whirl of a sophisticated Edinburgh circle, plus the activities into which her father had drawn her.

He had done so with a purpose; to ensure that she didn't become embroiled too much in the pleasure-seeking round which could be the inevitable lot of a girl educated at a fashionable school. He had been the leaven in her life — but it had taken his death to make her realize it.

Her eyelids drooped heavily, partly through the after-effect of sleeping-pills and partly because she was unwilling to face reality, but knowing that she had to and that Angus was urging her to.

With an effort she thrust her long legs out of bed, her feet groping for the mules which she usually kicked off at random and found at random, but now they were placed neatly, like a pair of sentinels standing side by side, so that when her feet searched ineffectively she looked down and saw the neat precision of the white slippers, and remembered that Bruce had placed them there.

As she pulled a matching white robe about her, she remembered his kindness and solicitude of the night before. He had wanted to take her to her father's house and put her in the care of the housekeeper, Mrs. McFee, but that was something she had been unable to face. The old house breathed of Angus; everything about it reflected his personality.

So, unwillingly and anxiously because he felt she shouldn't be left alone, Bruce had driven her home to the flat she occupied in a converted Georgian house in Moray Place. His own house was a couple of minutes away, and she had only to telephone, he said, and he would be around at the double. Then he had called her doctor, who came along and gave her something to make her sleep. After that, she remembered no more because a curtain had dropped over her mind, suddenly and mercifully.

She saw now that it was ten o'clock. Morning sunshine bathed the world outside. The quiet dignity of this part of Edinburgh's New Town reached out to her, but brought no comfort because suddenly it seemed desolate and empty without Erik's intimate companionship and her father's personality.

Angus himself had clung to his place in the Old Town, in a narrow street off the Royal Mile, but to walk from there down the broad sweep of the Mound, across Prince's Street and up to Charlotte Street then into Moray Place, had been a favorite jaunt of his. At one time he had done it whenever the mood took him, knowing she would always have his favorite snack of Gammon-and-Crowdie rolls waiting for him at the end of it, but after Erik came into her life he had taken the precaution of telephoning beforehand in case they were together.

With an effort, Margaret went along to

the kitchen, where she found a breakfast tray laid. She guessed at once that Bruce had S.O.S.d Mrs. McFee, who had been around while she slept. Beside the tray lay a note saying that Mrs. McFee would come back later to tidy up, so she was keeping the spare key.

Margaret was touched. She could picture the faithful soul plodding her way across from the Old Town, putting the needs of Angus Buchanan's daughter before her own. The woman had served Angus devotedly for many years.

As Margaret reached for the coffee-grinder, the telephone rang.

"I didn't want to wake you too soon."

It was Bruce, and she assured him he had not, and that she was grateful for all he had done. He brushed that aside. "I hope you've had something to eat?"

"I was going to make some coffee when you rang."

"Have some food as well. I've checked with Mrs. McFee about supplies. You mustn't neglect yourself. I'll be along soon."

"Not yet — "

She spoke too quickly, and was sorry,

but she wanted no one's company. Her senses craved the grace of solitude, time in which to stave off the responsibility of living. But that responsibility was already with her. The long day had begun, with its demand on her endurance.

"Please understand, Bruce — I'm all right, but I want to be left alone."

He was understanding, as always, but made her promise to call him as soon as she felt up to it, adding that he would be around later in any case. "Perhaps you'll feel like a quiet lunch at the Roxburghe, and then straight home."

How like him to choose the Roxburghe — discreet, genteel, and not far to walk. She could almost hear the way Bruce's mind ticked. He was anxious to protect her, to help her. There was no one else left in her life and he was quietly and efficiently taking over.

She knew she should express gratitude, but could only murmur a mechanical agreement, scarcely aware of what she said.

Bruce went on, "The doctor left some pills — you'll find them in the drawer beside your bed. Two every four hours, but no more."

He didn't have to tell her that, she thought with faint irritation. He should know well enough that she wasn't the type to do anything foolish.

She promised to take a couple if she needed them, thanked him again for all he had done, added that lunch at the Roxburghe sounded a good idea, but not that she had little appetite for it.

She had scarcely hung up before the doorbell sounded. The postman had some letters and an air-mail parcel bearing Norwegian stamps. She put the letters with others which had accumulated in her absence, and which she had not read. The parcel she put on a small Sheraton table, unwilling to open it, then picked it up, studied it, and put it down again. The writing was unfamiliar, so it could be nothing Angus had mailed to her before his death.

She turned and went along to the kitchen again, her limbs dragging in the aftermath of heavy and induced sleep, then changed her mind and went into the bathroom and took a shower, first hot, then cold, until her senses began to clear. Then she wrapped the white robe tightly about her and returned to the kitchen, made coffee and, remembering her promise to Bruce, some toast as well. She took the tray along to her bedroom and left it there while she went back for the mail — and the parcel.

And still she didn't open it. Not until last. It was as if some inner awareness knew that it contained her father's most personal possessions.

She was right. She took them out one by one: his worn spectacle case with the familiar horn-rims inside; his passport, bearing a very bad likeness but one which made her heart wrench; the bunch of keys he was always losing and sending Mrs. McFee to scour the house for; and then invariably finding in one of his cluttered pockets; his wallet, containing money in sterling and kroner; a photograph of her mother, young and gentle and smiling — Nina, who had died so inexplicably that doctors had been unable to diagnose her illness.

For the first time since hearing of her father's death, Margaret wept. Grief surged in great, tearing sobs, and when at last it was over she lay spent, his ancient wallet clutched in her hands, the leather smooth and worn to the touch, with that masculine smell about it which brought him right into the room.

She turned, then, to the rest; a diary, a memo pad, tickets for his return flight, various odds and ends, and a sealed, slightly bulging envelope. She opened it curiously, and the object within fell with a small thud into her lap.

It was a ring bearing an image of Varuna, the all-seeing one.

8

SHE sat rigid with her eyes closed. The ring was a dead weight in her hand, and almost as if he were in the room she heard the guru saying, '*But you will see it, Mrs. Drummond. Believe me, you will.*'

The words echoed through her brain, precisely enunciated by a voice to whom English was not a native tongue, and then on a further wave of shock the same voice was echoing through vast emptiness, advancing and retreating through a roar of sputtering static, rising to a crescendo until it shrieked in her ears, '*Mr. Sorenson is dead . . .*'

Her eyes flew open. She clutched the ring in a hand which shook, and through her stunned brain the voices still echoed as one — the voice of the guru in the temple above Katmandu, and the stranger in distant Norway. Identical voices, with the same precise accents and careful enunciation, the one warning her of trouble and the other bringing it. The one making predictions, and the other fulfilling them.

The fear which had been with her ever since her visit to the temple, and which had haunted her with increasing intensity as shock after shock pursued her, now soared to terrifying proportions. Even here, in the safety of her home, the thread of circumstance seemed to be weaving an inexorable pattern, remorselessly following her across the world.

She held her robe about her tightly, the ring pressing into the palm of her hand. She could feel the sharp edge of it, just as she had felt it when shaking hands with the man in the temple, and her palm jerked open and the face upon the ivory stared up at her, primitive, grotesque, the eyes closed — the eyes of Varuna, the all-seeing one, who could see through darkness as well as light — see all things and all people.

She began to pace the room, desperately trying to clutch at sanity so that she could think clearly and, please God, sensibly. She had forced herself to do so when the shock of Erik's death had urged her to rush back to the temple to challenge the man, to ask how he had known that a crisis was imminent. Only one thing had prevented her: the knowledge that he had been wrong about the ring.

Logically, that proved he was not infallible, even that he was a fraud, but logic deserted her now because the ring was here, in her hand, the enigmatic face of the god staring up at her, defying disbelief.

Margaret sank down upon a window seat and stared unseeingly across the rooftops of the ancient city, across the neighboring buildings of gray Edinburgh stone to that distant network of streets in the Old Town, courts and closes to which the entries were no more than dark slits where ghosts walked single file. But here, in this light and luxurious flat where such things as hauntings could never take place, the unseen presence of a far away mystic seemed to be reminding her of his uncanny predictions.

With whose mind had he communicated to gather such knowledge? Who had sent the warnings? What fantastic flight of thought had winged its way from a remote region of Norway to a remote region in distant Nepal? Certainly its source had not been Angus Buchanan. Predictions, astrology, fortune-telling, spiritualism — her father never had time for such things. So the guru must have been in touch with someone else who knew precisely when disaster struck. If mind-projection over vast distances was really possible, this was the only explanation.

Margaret turned away from the window and saw the opened package lying where she had left it. Odd, she thought, that no note accompanied it. She studied the wrapping but all it revealed was a label bearing her own name and address — no indication of the sender, no return address in case of non-delivery.

She tossed the wrapping aside, and something fell out and rolled across the floor.

It was a sealed container, enclosing a cassette of film.

She picked it up and studied it curiously. Why had the sender, whoever he was, enclosed this? Was it something Angus had been experimenting with, or a film which contained particularly valuable shots? Her brow creased in a puzzled frown. There must be a reason for air-mailing one particular film.

But whatever the reason, it could not be dealt with now. She would go to her father's laboratory to process it later. The idea of working there without him was painful, but, like everything else, had to be faced. Meanwhile there was lunch with Bruce. It would be her first attempt at picking up the threads of living again.

She put the film on her dressing table tray, but put the Varuna ring into her handbag. For some reason she wanted to keep it close beside her.

★ ★ ★

Lunch, after all, was a mistake. She sat through it in a daze, half listening to Bruce's conversation, her mind constantly turning to the film. The more she thought about it the more significant it seemed and the more anxious she became to find out what it revealed.

Despite her inattentiveness, Bruce was patient and kind. This was a side of his nature she had never suspected. She had always seen him as an aloof, self-sufficient man, his character steeled by the tragedy in his life, but now she realized that behind the cold exterior lay a warmth which was touching in its unexpectedness. For this reason she suddenly found herself confiding in him about the package and the film it contained.

"I can't wait to see what is in it," she finished, and then fell silent because Bruce was looking at her, saying nothing, and she knew at once that he believed she had imagined the whole thing.

Nor was she really surprised. Bruce knew, as well as she, that Angus had taken a quantity of films with him, all of which would eventually arrive with his photographic equipment. So it just didn't make sense that some anonymous person should air-mail one isolated film. She would have to show it to Bruce in order to convince him.

She was silent during the short walk back to her flat, but when they reached it Bruce wouldn't come in. He advised her to take another tranquillizer and rest, then kissed her gently on the cheek and left. Margaret went straight to her bedroom, the film very much on her mind, but when she reached for it her outstretched hand came to an abrupt halt.

The film was not there.

After searching without success she stood staring at the silver toilet tray on which she had placed the film. The blank space stared back at her and she turned abruptly, opened the drawer beside her bed, tipped a couple of pills into the palm of her shaking hand, and went along to the kitchen for a glass of water. After taking the pills she kicked off her shoes and lay down on the bed, pulling a throw over her.

After a while she began to relax, but kept drowsiness at bay by staring across the room at her dressing table, almost willing the film to reappear. Beside the silver tray, on the polished walnut surface of the dressing table, was a brooch which she had accidentally knocked aside when putting the film down.

That was no dream. Nor was the Varuna ring. Margaret tossed the throw aside and reached for her hand-bag; the ring was there, safe and sound. She wished now that she had told Bruce about that as well, but she had given it no thought because the matter of the film had occupied her mind. In any case, the ring would have meant nothing to him. He would merely have dismissed it as some barbaric curio her father had picked up on his travels.

Suddenly the recollection of Mrs. McFee's note leaped into Margaret's mind; the woman had said she would be along later to tidy up . . .

In a flash Margaret reached for the phone and, as she listened to the distant ringing, thought with impatient amusement of what Mrs. McFee's tidying-up usually meant. Angus had always complained that he could never find a thing afterwards.

In a moment the housekeeper was saying with pride that she had seen the film on the toilet tray, " . . . so for safety I put it in that antique tea-caddy on your desk in the living room."

Margaret thanked her weakly, too relieved to utter reproach. She added that she would be coming along to the house later. Mrs. McFee replied that she was just leaving to catch a bus to Portobello to visit her sister, but she would wait in if Margaret wanted her to.

"Of course not — I'll let myself in, and perhaps you'll return before I leave."

Margaret replaced the receiver and flopped back upon the bed. She wished devoutly that she had not taken the pills because now she was really feeling drowsy and would have to sleep it off before going along to her father's lab. But at least she had proof that she had not dreamed the whole thing.

★ ★ ★

When she wakened it was late evening, and uppermost in her mind was the conviction that the film was significant, as if her father were commanding her to give it special and immediate attention.

After a quick shower she dressed hurriedly, pulling on the first thing that came to hand, then she collected the film from Mrs. McFee's hiding-place and put it safely in her handbag.

At the last moment she slipped the talisman ring on her finger. It was large, loose, and promptly fell off, so she thrust it onto her index finger and there it remained, not very comfortably because it was still too large — a man's ring, never intended for a female hand. It looked rather splendid, bronze and primitive against the coral linen of the trouser-suit she had picked at random.

She was leaving the flat when her telephone began to ring. She hesitated, then shut the front door firmly behind her and went on her way to collect her car from the garage in a narrow street behind the terrace. It was good to see the Singer Sports again, standing there like an old friend who had been neglected, but when she switched on the ignition the engine merely groaned in protest and refused to start.

"So you're sulking, are you," she muttered, "just because I've been away and left you alone?" The engine gave a deep sigh in answer, and died.

It was a good half-hour before the battery was recharged and she was able to drive up Charlotte Street then left into Prince's Street. The solid bulk of the castle stood high on its pile of once volcanic rock, towering above the ancient city, and against the twilit sky the irregular roofs and gables of the Lawnmarket looked like part of a theatrical set.

The familiar view caught her heart, as always, as she skirted the Prince's Street gardens then swooped right up the Mound and into the Royal Mile, St. Giles's Cathedral standing in blackened dignity at the entrance to High Street, which formed the central part of the famous thoroughfare. She could see the long, picturesque, historical stretch ahead of her, with the Palace of Holyroodhouse at the end and, as the Singer rumbled over ancient cobblestones, the dusky fingers of evening probed the narrow slits of sinister courts, shadowy closes, and twisting stone stairs which led upward to cheek-by-jowl tenement flats.

This was the heart of ancient Edinburgh, where once the aristocracy had lived, and which had deteriorated rapidly into a slum area with the coming of the New Town, but now it was rising again, becoming the home of intellectuals and students and men like Angus Buchanan.

High Street merged into the Canongate, the longest stretch of the Royal Mile, and here Margaret parked her car, then walked through the dark archway leading into St. John's Street. Ancient iron posts at each end of the arch barred entry to all but pedestrians, and for the first time in her life she found herself hurrying through the shadowy approach, startled by the echo of her own footsteps. A wind was gathering, blowing in chilly gusts between the old stone walls.

Mrs. McFee often swore that the ghosts of the Knights of St. John, who had once inhabited the close, still lingered here, their crusader wounds tormenting them, their heads battered and bloodied. The whispering sound of centuries seemed to haunt the dark entry, and Margaret continued to hurry until emerging into the dimly-lit close. Her footsteps still echoed with a hollow sound as she covered the few remaining yards to her father's house, which stood back behind a small garden on the right.

As she fumbled in her handbag for

the key, a sudden lump rose in her throat. It seemed impossible that this narrow street would never again echo to Angus's heavy tread, that he would never again push open the wrought-iron gate and stride up the short path to the ancient front door.

The house dated back to the early sixteenth-century, and still retained many of its original features, including a secret escape passage at the rear, hewn between stone walls six feet thick, leaving a cavity so narrow that only one man could pass through at a time and if an enemy were confronted it was a case of kill or be killed.

History breathed within the old house and Angus had taken a justifiable pride in the place, retaining its character and atmosphere. At the same time, he had stamped his own personality upon it, so much so that as Margaret stepped into the raftered hall she almost expected him to walk through the door leading from his study, or to call out to her as he always did when he heard her come in.

Instead, all that met her was a heavy, brooding silence.

She closed the front door behind her firmly, called to Mrs. McFee in the kitchen and, receiving no reply, knew that the woman had not yet returned. She was alone in the still house, and suddenly a feeling of oppression weighed upon her; a sense of foreboding.

She thrust it aside determinedly and walked down the passage leading to the laboratory. One of her father's most forcible protests, when suggestions were made that he should move into a more pretentious part of the city, was that no other laboratory would suit him so well as the one he had here.

The rear ground-floor rooms had been converted several years ago, and expanded as his experiments increased, and if people considered it odd that a man so successful should cling to an area which anyone with his means would have left long ago, he didn't care in the least. He had lived here for years and here, he always declared, he would die.

Besides, he insisted, he *liked* the old street, and the picturesque district, and the varying types of people who inhabited it. They didn't bother him, they even liked him, so why should he face moving just to keep up with the Joneses? He didn't like that strata of society which 'The Joneses' made up.

A pig-headed and sometimes difficult man, but such characteristics were to be expected in so individual a person. Margaret felt a strong nostalgia for him as she opened the door of his laboratory.

The place was small, but splendidly equipped, perfect for Angus to experiment and work in. The factory which produced the end-product of his brain, financed by Bruce Matheson, was in an outer industrial suburb. Angus had left the running of that to Bruce, shares in the business being split three ways — one-third to Matheson, one-third to himself, one-third to his daughter.

Margaret flung off her jacket and, as she did so, something clattered to the floor and rolled away. It was the ring. She picked it up and dropped it into her handbag, at the same time taking out the roll of film.

In recent months Angus had become more and more absorbed in perfecting this emulsion-coated product, by which he had increased its sensitivity to a subject. His work had become of tremendous value to the government in the area of long-range photography from the air, but this film was an even greater step forward, its surface so sensitive that photographs could be taken, sharply and clearly, in excessively dim light without the aid of flash or infra-red.

Margaret switched on every light in the laboratory. The brilliance seemed to keep at bay the illusion that she was not alone. Even here, in this sparkling, modern, scientifically equipped room, she had sometimes sensed an atmosphere which no amount of modernization could overcome. In imaginative moments she felt that it emanated from the secret passage which led straight out of the laboratory by means of a sliding panel in the wall.

The adjoining darkroom was as up-to-date as the lab, but Margaret knew that processing the film would involve moments when all light would have to be eliminated no matter how fraught her nerves might be, and for a fleeting second she wished that she had waited until tomorrow, or that Mrs. McFee would return so that comforting sounds of her presence could be heard from the distant kitchen.

She briskly pulled on an overall, picked up the film, and took it into the darkroom. At this stage light was a necessity and, behind her, the brilliance of the laboratory was reassuring. Within moments the routine of work absorbed her and her nerves steadied. She poured developer into a tank, then loaded the film into a spiral ready to hand. After that, she closed the intervening door, shutting out the glare of the lab, then returned to the work table and found that she had to steel herself to touch a light switch above her head and plunge the room into total darkness.

For a brief, unnerved second she stood still, then her hands moved automatically, putting the film into the tank and covering it. Then she switched on the overhead light again and began to agitate the tank so that the film was completely immersed.

On a deep breath she said aloud,

"*Now*," and once more switched off the light.

Removing the lid from the tank, she took out the film, then the noise of running water filled the silent room as she rinsed it, followed by the sound of the spiral being placed in a separate tank of rapid fixer. Fifteen seconds, no more. She timed them by the luminous dial of her watch, each second seeming as long as a minute.

And as she stood there in the dark, she heard a sound from beyond the wall which concealed the secret passage. She gave an involuntary start, then reminded herself that old houses such as this were always full of noises.

She kept her eyes on the luminous dial until the fifteen seconds were up, then she switched on the light again, unwound the film, and started on the requisite ten minutes' washing. After that she carried the length of exposure to the drying cabinet, and switched on.

Another ten minutes and she would see, in negative form, what the film revealed.

To pass the time, she went to the

laboratory. She was conscious of an increasing tension and uncannily convinced that the film contained something at which she could not even guess and was almost afraid to see.

She gave a sudden jump, startled again by a noise from the secret passage. It sounded like the movement of feet and she felt a lurch of apprehension. Then she forced it down and crossed briskly to the hidden panel.

It moved slowly and with difficulty because of disuse, but when at last it was open the brilliant lights from the laboratory revealed nothing — merely a dusty stone passage curving out of sight, following a bend in the outer wall.

Vexed with herself for being so fanciful, Margaret closed the panel again. Now everywhere was quiet; the house, the laboratory, the darkroom beyond. The whole place seemed to hold its breath, as if the ghosts of generations who had lived here stood close beside her, watching, staring, waiting with her as the minutes ticked away.

Five to go. She had never before noticed how loudly her little watch ticked. Four minutes. It was slowing down — she was sure it was slowing down. She held it to her ear and the steady ticking mocked her.

Three . . . two . . . one . . . zero . . .

She hurried back into the darkroom, and after switching off the drying cabinet she opened it and saw the film hanging suspended, twenty exposures in color.

Now her brows met in a puzzled frown and her tension subsided a little beneath a sudden curiosity, for there seemed to be little color — mostly darkness, with blobs of light.

Faces? People? She couldn't tell, but it was suddenly vital that she should.

Her hands moved swiftly then, cutting the film into strips of five, and as she worked she studied the tiny negatives, but with exposures taken against so dark a background it was impossible to see much detail at this stage.

Impelled now by an overriding urgency she put the negatives into an enlarger and saw every detail projected onto the baseboard, blown up to nearly a foot square. Her forehead creased in greater bewilderment. What she saw didn't make sense. It looked like a picture of some macabre drama.

She hurried to run off a quick print of one, to see the picture in the positive, to convince herself that what she imagined she saw was due solely to the dim and indecipherable background. For this she selected a picture in closeup; a face in the foreground, others in the background. She worked rapidly, almost as if racing against time and the fear of intrusion.

Slowly, the picture appeared; shadowy at first, then suddenly leaping to life. She recoiled, swayed, and the room whirled about her. She realized that she was looking at a picture of macabre rites following the celebration of a Black Mass; orgiastic, fiendish, with figures contorted in bestial ritual, dominated by one demented with evil lust; the face was monstrous and malevolent, but terrifyingly familiar. Darkness threatened to engulf her, but through it the face in the picture stared back. She closed her eyes against it, but the truth and the shock were inescapable.

It was a long time before she could bring herself to take hold of the horrifying print and place it, with the remaining negatives, in protective transparent paper. Her instinct was to burn the lot. Instead, she put all into a folder and took them with her, and there was a deep sickness in her heart as she left the house.

Minutes later, in the deserted laboratory, the panel in the wall opened slowly and from the secret passage a figure stepped out.

9

AS Mrs. McFee plodded downstairs, the front doorbell rang impatiently. She hurried to open it, and Bruce Matheson almost brushed her aside as he entered, announcing that he had been around to Mrs. Drummond's flat and could get no reply. Telephoning brought no reply either, so he presumed she was here.

"I'm afraid not, sir." The housekeeper added soothingly that perhaps Mrs. Drummond had merely gone out for some fresh air.

Then she had been out a long time, Bruce reflected. He had followed up his telephone call of the night before with another from his office at around ten o'clock, fully expecting a reply. At that hour Margaret would normally have been up and about, breakfast long finished, but he had allowed a margin for late sleep in the present circumstances.

After two more calls he had had the line

checked. Everything was normal, but the subscriber did not reply. He telephoned again at regular intervals and each time the hollow ring sounded mocking in his ears.

At eleven-thirty there was a Board Meeting which, as Chairman, he had to attend, but his secretary had instructions to keep calling and to check that Mrs. Drummond was all right.

The Board Meeting was long and tedious, and at the end of it there was still no reply from Margaret's number, so he left his office as early as possible and drove straight to her flat, where he listened to the doorbell echoing through silent rooms while his anxiety mounted to apprehension. Then, obeying an instinct, he had driven straight here.

He heard Mrs. McFee saying, "Last I heard from Mrs. Drummond was when she telephoned yesterday sir."

He asked sharply, "What time was that?"

"After lunch, sir, just before I left for my sister's out at Portobello. She'd asked me over because she didn't think I should be left alone here."

131

Matheson threw Mrs. McFee an impatient glance; one which said plainly that *she* wasn't the person who shouldn't be left alone. His concern for Margaret was so plain that the woman's ruffled feelings subsided. She was genuinely sorry she had not waited in, and said so. "But she sounded so much more like herself, sir, especially when I set her mind at rest about the film."

Bruce, who had been glancing idly down the long passage leading to the laboratory, spun around at that. "Film? What film?"

"One she'd left on her dressing table, sir. I'd been around to tidy up, so of course I told her where I'd put it — but of all things to worry about at a time like this, a little thing like a film!"

"And what did she say when you told her?"

"That she might be around later, but I wasn't to wait in."

To the woman's astonishment, Bruce said furiously, "And you didn't try to *stop* her?"

The housekeeper bridled at that.

"How could I, sir? She has her own key."

"The last place Mrs. Drummond should visit just now is her father's house. She must not be allowed to brood over his death."

Then how about her being cooped up in that flat, brooding over the death of the man she was in love with? Mrs. McFee was tempted to ask. Wasn't that bad for her too? But a good housekeeper knew her place, so she merely inclined her head respectfully.

Bruce took a worried pace or two, then asked, "So you don't know whether she came around or not?"

"No, sir, but when I got back I must say it didn't look as if she'd been in the house at all. She always headed straight for her father's study; if he was out, she'd make herself some coffee and take it along there."

The woman's rambling explanation irritated Bruce, but he checked the reaction, remembering that she was getting on; remembering, too, that she had hurried around to Moray Place without protest to see what she could do; remembering her devotion to both Angus Buchanan and his daughter.

"Did you look in the laboratory, Mrs. McFee?"

"Oh, no, sir. Mr. Buchanan never liked me going in there. Wouldn't let me tidy up or anything — only himself or Mrs. Drummond. You know what he's like, sir." She corrected herself unhappily, "Was like, I mean."

Bruce touched her arm sympathetically, and confided, "I'm worried, Mrs. McFee. Do you happen to have a key to Mrs. Drummond's flat?"

To his relief, the woman said she had. "I keep it for when she goes away, sir, so that I can keep an eye on the place."

"Yes, yes — bring it to me."

"Oh, sir, you don't think there's anything — *wrong*?"

"I don't know. Just bring me that key. Meanwhile, I'll take a quick look at the lab."

When the woman came bustling back, Bruce was coming down the passage from the laboratory. "Not a sign," he said, and took the key with a word of thanks.

134

"Would you like me to come along with you, sir, in case there's anything I can do?"

His only answer was a shake of the head as he hurried from the house.

As soon as Bruce entered Margaret's flat, he knew it was deserted. It had the atmosphere of a place which had been shut up all day, windows closed, rooms stuffy and airless, letters still on the hall mat.

He picked them up mechanically and put them on the Sheraton table which Angus had given Margaret when she took this place after her divorce. Somehow Bruce had expected her to go back home to the house in St. John's Street, since she was now working daily in the laboratory, but Angus had felt differently. It was natural and right that his daughter should want a place of her own.

It was Bruce who had found this flat for her; they were not readily available in this expensive area, but he knew whom to approach and how to go about things. It had pleased him to have Margaret living so near, with young Drummond safely in the past and no other man in her future.

Wisely, or so he had thought, he decided not to rush her — and that was one of the few decisions in his life which he regretted.

Standing in the hall, he called her name, announcing himself as a precaution, then glanced into the living room and kitchen, both deserted, and finally going along to the bedroom. The nearly made-up bed confirmed, at least, that she was not ill.

In a way, he was disappointed, because he was anxious not to let her out of his sight. He had been worried by her manner at lunch yesterday, and by the things she had said, although he had taken care not to show it. Even her assurance later, on the telephone, that she was all right and that he was not to concern himself about her had failed to convince him. Since the breakup of her marriage Margaret had learned how to hide her feelings. One never really knew what she was thinking, so reserved had she become.

Except with Sorenson, he thought resentfully. The man had not merely broken through her reserve, but swept it aside, wasting no time on slow and patient wooing.

The kitchen told Bruce little, except that her breakfast things were in the dishwasher, clean and dry. Sometimes she waited until the dishes from a later meal could be added, then did the lot together, but this morning she had switched it on as if it were her last meal of the day. She only did that if she were eating out for the rest of it, or going away. He knew her habits more intimately than she realized.

The living room revealed nothing more than a cigarette stub in the ash tray beside the telephone. The room gave the distinct impression of not having been used otherwise.

On his way back to the bedroom Bruce glanced at her morning mail, but it consisted of nothing more than a few inland first-class letters and second-class bills. What worried him was the fact that she had not bothered to pick them up.

The only interpretation to be put upon that was that she had gone out before the postal delivery. It came between eight and eight-thirty, on the same round as Heriot Row.

He moved swiftly to the bedroom. It was reasonably tidy, but some crumpled tissue paper lay on the floor, screwed into a long roll, the way his wife had stuffed sleeves when packing, then pulling the tissue out and casting it aside when unpacking. Paula usually threw all tissue paper back into the suitcases, ready for re-use, but sometimes odd pieces got left behind in hotel rooms after departure. This discarded piece seemed to suggest the same thing.

Now thoroughly agitated, Bruce crossed to the dressing table. An empty film container lay discarded, its black plastic lid also cast aside. Apart from this, the table told him nothing. He pulled open the two small drawers at the top, where most women kept cosmetics. There were none.

He was more than ever convinced that Margaret had gone away, and a quick inspection of her wardrobe confirmed it. Her clothes were kept in long cupboards which occupied the whole of one wall, winter and summer clothes divided by a rising tier of sliding trays. He was faced on one side with winter suits and coats, stored in sealed transparent covers, and on the other with a few dresses and evening gowns, plus a couple of rejected trouser-suits which looked as if she had pulled them out, changed her mind, and thrust them back again. After that came a wide gap stocked only with empty hangers.

Bruce's quick eye detected that her climbing kit was missing. That clinched everything and he scarcely glanced at the sliding trays, except to observe that underwear had been removed, leaving two trays completely empty.

A final glance at the long top shelf which ran the whole width of the cupboards confirmed that the airplane luggage she always used when flying, and which he had stacked into the trunk of his car at the airport only the other night, was also missing.

His mind worked rapidly then, and as it did so he moved about the room, searching for any indication of where she might have gone. There was nothing but that empty tin which had once contained a cassette of film. It was surely the film she had told him about, the one which had come so mysteriously from Norway and about which she had telephoned Mrs. McFee. He had pretended not to heed Margaret's story about the film. He had thought it undesirable that she should be worried by a reminder of her father, but he had paid attention, nevertheless.

He glanced into the waste-paper basket, but it yielded no useful information. He then hurried to the kitchen, remembering that Mrs. McFee had tidied up the day before. No discarded wrapping paper would escape her diligent eye — and sure enough, in the large wastebin was some torn brown paper bearing Norwegian stamps. He could just discern the postmark — *Voshanger, Norge.*

Those stamps were like a signpost, pointing.

As Bruce was leaving the building he saw the porter in his lodge.

Mrs. Drummond? Yes, she had gone out early, very early.

"I come on at eight, sir, and she already had her car at the door. I carried her bags down, sir, while she fetched a traveling coat and locked up. Traveling light, she was, but she had her camera, of course. Never goes on a trip without that, does she, sir?"

No, she hadn't said where she was going, and he was very sorry, but he hadn't thought it was his place to ask. Mrs. Drummond was always taking off for somewhere or other, and then coming back again, suddenlike.

Bruce went on to Heriot Row, slamming his front door behind him as he headed for the phone. But at the airport he drew a blank. The counterfoils of bookings for both Heathrow and Gatwick had gone through to Administration, and that included Desk Bookings. Administration was closed now, but if he called back tomorrow they might be able to trace a particular booking, providing he produced the necessary authority for a search to be made.

Bruce slammed down the receiver. Whichever way he turned, he seemed to meet up with a blank wall. He felt as if he were stumbling in the dark, and in a fury of frustration he rang for Wallace. There were several messages, but none from Mrs. Drummond. The manservant poured Bruce his usual Scotch-and-soda, asked if he would be in for dinner, and received curt instructions to bring something cold on a tray as soon as possible.

Alone, Bruce thought hard. A journey without a motive or goal was uncharacteristic of Margaret, so she would not have obeyed some wild impulse to run away from everything. And then there was the empty film container — with no sign of its contents in either the flat or the laboratory. His inspection of both had been thorough.

He knew the routine work of film processing. Newly developed films were always hung up in the lab, or even left hanging in the drying cabinet after switching off, but there was no trace of a newly developed film in either. The only indication of work being done were a couple of upturned tanks on the drainer in the dark room, tanks which had contained developer and fixer, rinsed after use and left to drain.

Both had been dry, which meant that they could have been there since the previous night — or since the last lot of work was completed prior to Angus's departure.

But Angus had been meticulous about leaving everything in its place, the laboratory spick and span, before departing on a trip.

When Wallace wheeled in the dinner trolly, Bruce was on the phone, booking a first class flight to Norway later that night.

"To Oslo *or* Bergen, whichever leaves first!"

His voice sounded tense and Wallace was surprised. His master's trips to Scandinavia were frequent, because his business interests there were demanding, but they were never as urgent as this one sounded.

He waited discreetly until the telephone conversation ended, then asked, "Do you wish me to pack your bags, sir? For how long, sir? A few days?"

"Indefinitely," Bruce answered shortly. "I'm catching the late night flight out of Edinburgh, so you'd better look sharp."

Wallace was too experienced a man-servant to linger when his employer was as worried as he appeared to be now.

143

After eating his meal, Bruce sat tossing the empty film container thoughtfully in his hand, thinking back over his lunch-time meeting with Margaret. He went over every detail in his mind, from the moment when she had opened her front door to him to the time he took her back from the Roxburghe and insisted on her resting again.

He felt that somewhere along the line there should be something to indicate her intention to go out later. Had she kept quiet because she knew he would try to dissuade her?

The thought distressed him. He had taken charge of her with an authority to which she had submitted ever since he had met her on her arrival home, and this submission had pleased him. But now he was worried.

Slipping around to her father's house, secretly, to develop that film — as he was now convinced she had done — without even hinting that she planned to do so, indicated that her submission was not total.

He was deeply perturbed.

10

THE hotel at Voshanger over-
looked the fjord, with gardens
sweeping down to the water's
edge, and chalets for guests, and moorings
for boats. Margaret chose a chalet rather
than a room in the main building because
she still wanted solitude and a cabin
among the pines offered greater privacy
as well as being quieter.

The hotel itself, built entirely of timber,
was like a country house in typical
Norwegian style, with carved balconies
and a multitude of flowering plants at
windows and steps. It stood in the center
of the village, its front facing the main
street which linked with the fjord road
at each end, and the rear of the hotel
over-looked gardens and a stretch of water
leading from the mainstream.

The interior of the hotel was paneled in
unbleached pine, with carved balustrades
— 'hand-made by local craftsmen,' said
the brochure — and had she been

145

feeling more relaxed, Margaret would have studied the beautiful woodwork with interest. As it was, she flicked over the pages of the brochure politely, hardly taking in the text, and paying little attention to the woman at the reception desk who had handed her the booklet.

The woman spoke English well. Everyone spoke English well. That much at least had registered since Margaret's arrival in Bergen, and during the trip by steamer into the Hardanger Fjord, the only fjord south of the ancient port.

At any other time, in any other circumstances, she would have been impressed by the grandeur of the scene, for the Hardanger presented every aspect of Norway, from white-capped mountains to sweeping forests, cascading waterfalls descending thousands of feet to empty the mineral content of glaciers into the smooth waters below, and toy villages which, in the spring, would stand amidst acres of cherry-blossom orchards, but throughout the journey she had been intent only on her purpose in coming here.

The boat trip to this offshoot from the

main fjord had seemed the longest part, despite the fact that it was enlivened by glimpses of logging camps. Forestry seemed to be a flourishing industry here, which surprised her, for she had always understood that it was confined to the eastern side of the country.

The hotel manageress was pushing the register towards her, and Margaret realized that the woman was not only saying something but looking at her intently as if repeating a remark and wondering if she had not been heard. Margaret glanced up in apology, noting for the first time how attractive the woman was — middle-aged but elegant, with looks which many a man would notice.

"I was wondering if this was your first visit to Norway?"

"Yes, my first," Margaret jerked, and pulled off her glove to sign the register. Promptly the talisman ring, large and loose on her finger, shot across the reception desk and onto the floor behind. It had been foolish to wear it, but she had slipped it on before leaving Edinburgh and there it had remained — until now.

The manageress stooped to retrieve it, and when Margaret laid aside the pen she noticed how pale the woman was. Perhaps naturally so. Beneath soft brown hair the skin was very light. Beyond that, Margaret paid little attention to her. She held out her hand for the ring, saying politely that she would like to go to her room at once.

"Of course — right away."

The manageress rang for a porter and when Margaret picked up her camera in its distinctive case the woman said, "Olaf can take that too — " then broke off. She stared at the camera case for a moment, then turned away and took a key from a row of hooks behind her.

"Tell Olaf to bring these bags to Chalet Seventeen," she instructed a clerk — the clerk to whom Margaret had spoken on the phone from Frankfurt? — then she led the way out of the hotel, down a short flight of wooden steps and across sweeping lawns to a copse of trees overlooking the fjord.

"My name is Thorsen," she said. "Sonja Thorsen. I took the job of manageress here ten years ago. Before that I was in Oslo."

Margaret made a polite, interested sort of noise. She was in no mood for conversation, even if this Norwegian woman was. She followed automatically as Sonja Thorsen led her down a gravel path and up a couple of steps to the small veranda of a chalet with 17 above its door, and the thought struck Margaret that perhaps Angus himself had occupied this very cabin during one of his visits. He had always stayed at the Voshanger Hotel, until this last trip, so the woman who ran the place must have met him often.

On his last visit too? Even though he had not stayed here, he might well have dropped in for a drink or a meal. Had she met him then? Had she spoken to him shortly before he died?

Questions thronged Margaret's mind — demanding, urgent. 'Did you know my father? You must have — he stayed here often enough. What about his last visit? Where could he have stayed, if not at this hotel? Did you see him around the village? Did he come here at all? Did you talk with him? Did you talk with him before he died? That very day, that very night?' But the questions remained unspoken. This was not the time.

Sonja Thorsen unlocked the chalet door and stepped aside for Margaret to enter.

"Olaf will be down with your bags in a minute or two. Would you like anything meanwhile — some tea, perhaps? With milk, or lemon? Or you may have drinks served here, unless you prefer the bar."

They stood looking at each other, and still Margaret couldn't say a word. She wasn't yet ready to talk about her father, and even reluctant to think about him, because now she was here, in the place where he had been killed — too many disturbing pictures came between her mind and her words, pictures which posed terrifying questions which were perhaps better left unspoken.

A little time, only a little time, that was all she needed, and then she would be ready to talk to anyone. She needed time in which to get adjusted, time to look around.

She insisted on this to herself, but knew it was untrue. She was being cowardly and evasive, afraid of the unknown, conscious of a creeping sense of fear which now reached out to her from the darkening mountains. It was somewhere here, in this actual vicinity, where that horrifying photograph had been taken.

And it was from here that the anonymous parcel had been sent. She had to find out the identity of the sender. That was the reason why she had come.

Sonja Thorsen said again, "Are you sure you wouldn't like some tea? We serve dinner early here, but after your journey you might be glad of some refreshment. You've come a long way."

Her smile was kind, adding sweetness to her attractive face.

"Thank you, Mrs. Thorsen. Tea would be lovely. With lemon, please."

"Miss Thorsen," the woman corrected with a smile. "I am unmarried."

Margaret was surprised. Even in her state of fatigue and the aftermath of shock she could not fail to realize that Sonja Thorsen was anything but a typical spinster. She was essentially a man's woman.

Sonja was about to close the door when she suddenly added, "If you need anything, or want anything, don't bother to call Reception, Mrs. Drummond. Please call me personally."

She gave a warm smile, and closed the door quietly behind her.

Margaret put her handbag and camera on a chair and, as she did so, she saw the initials A.B. on the camera case, very small and unobtrusive. The camera had been one of her father's before he had given it to her, and he identified all his equipment in this way. The lack of flamboyancy about the initialing was typical of his whole personality. Margaret put out a hand, touching the letters with a gentle finger, then dropped her coat on the same chair, lit a cigarette and lay down upon the bed.

She was in Voshanger at last, her mother's birthplace, and again she wondered why her father had never brought her here. It was true that she had no relatives on her mother's side; Nina had been an orphan when Angus met her, married her, and took her to Scotland to live, so there was no specific reason why she should visit her mother's home village or her mother's homeland — but, on the other hand, why not? She had Norwegian blood in her. Why should Angus have come continually to this place without her?

Uneasiness crept into the darkening room. Outside, night was drawing in and shadows slid through the windows. Pine trees shivered and the waters of the fjord whispered against the shore. Smoke curled up from Margaret's now unheeded cigarette. She lay rigid, the small room suddenly pressing in upon her, silent and menacing.

Equally suddenly, she was plunged into a blaze of light, and the shock of it brought a cry to her throat.

"Your bags, madam."

The cry died, unuttered. It was only the porter, beaming, telling her she shouldn't sit alone in the dark and that her tea would be along shortly.

Margaret stubbed out her cigarette with a shaking hand. Her nerves must be shot to pieces, to react like that.

"Don't bother about the tea," she said, "I'll go up to the hotel for a drink."

She had to get out of here; the chalet had become claustrophobic. She needed the sound of voices and the sight of people; she wanted to be with others, behaving in a sane and normal way in a sane and normal world, a world where there were no shadows and no fears, so that she could reassure herself that she was sane and normal too.

She flicked a comb through her hair, dabbed at her make-up and, in her haste, sent her large traveling handbag flying. The photograph folder, with its hideous contents, fell to the floor and she saw the white edge of a print — *the* print — projecting slightly.

It was that terrible thing which had brought her to this place. She had carried it with her throughout the journey, but now could stand it no longer. She swept it into a suitcase, burying it beneath clothes which she must later unpack, slamming the lid and relocking it.

Then, amongst the spilled contents of her bag, she saw the primitive face of Varuna, the all-seeing one, surveying her inscrutably.

"You're giving me the jitters, damn

you," she said aloud, and dropped the ring into a drawer and slammed it shut, then left the lights blazing as she went up to the hotel.

★ ★ ★

The bar was furnished with clean scrubbed tables and matching seats, the usual profusion of indoor plants adorning walls built of hand-hewn logs. The ceiling was beamed, and linked with the walls by a hand-carved frieze depicting Scandinavian gods, Vikings and their ships, trolls and legendary figures. Stools and chairbacks were also carved, and the whole place had a kind of folklore simplicity about it, warmed by a tiled Norwegian stove in a far corner.

Margaret chose a seat against a wall, in banquette style, running the full length of the wall and upholstered in a coarse folkweave in a traditional Norwegian pattern of reindeer, Laplanders, and mountain firs. She guessed that, like the carving, the weaving was of local workmanship, and this was confirmed by a notice beside the bar, for the benefit of tourists.

She ordered a Campari-soda, then looked around in disappointment. She had escaped from her chalet in search of human companionship, only to find the bar bereft of it. But it was early yet, so she allowed her thoughts to stray back to Edinburgh, and Bruce.

In a way, she regretted not telling him of her plans, but she had refrained in case he tried to prevent her from coming, or insisted on accompanying her. Apart from that, she would have had to reveal why she felt it essential to come to Voshanger and she was not yet ready to let anyone know the reason — except the sender of the film.

She had thrashed the whole thing out in her mind through the long night after she had returned from her father's laboratory. Apart from the intensity of earlier shocks, the final one of the photograph had rendered sleep out of the question. Even having the sinister picture in the flat had made her afraid of dropping off at all.

She had planned her departure carefully, checking on scheduled flights leaving for

156

Norway the next morning to tie up with one from Edinburgh, then forcing herself to pack methodically, and as she did so the telephone had rung. It had, of course, been Bruce, and for a moment the temptation to confide in him had been strong, but several things stopped her. The feeling that she had been enough trouble to him already, the knowledge that he would immediately start organizing her and, most deterring of all, the fact that she would have to show him the photograph with its damning revelation.

So she had merely assured him that she was fine, and there was no need to worry about her.

Now she wished that he were here. His companionship would have been comforting.

Her Campari arrived, and as she sipped it she saw her reflection in a wide mirror flanking the wall behind the bar. It was the first time she had really studied herself since hearing of her father's death. Even when applying make-up she had viewed her face without any real attention, but now it looked back at her — tired, strained and marked with distress.

Then behind her, also reflected in the mirror, she saw the bar entrance, at one moment empty and the next framing the figure of a man. His eyes met hers in the mirror and her heart froze instantly.

That dark head was unmistakable.

11

FOR a moment they stared at each other. The strip-lighting above the mirror was harsh, throwing back their reflections in unrelieved detail. She saw the hard craggy face, the face of the man in Frankfurt, and to her startled mind he seemed as menacing now as he had appeared then.

She turned away quickly, but the physical power of the man registered subconsciously beneath the frightening realization that he had finally tracked her down.

His heavy footsteps crossed the room and stopped beside her table. She was forced to look up, and he said with a touch of irony, "Perhaps you'll explain your behavior when we last met. I'd had a hell of a job tracing you through that fog, and when at last I succeeded you didn't even pause to ask where I'd found your passport."

"*Found it?*" she jerked.

"What else? You didn't imagine I'd stolen it, did you?" He added with amusement, "What use would a woman's passport be to me?"

She felt as if she were floundering between embarrassment and bewilderment, but she managed to ask, "Where did you find it?"

"You spilled the contents of your hand-bag onto the chair in the Frankfurterhof, but overlooked your passport. Naturally, I hurried after you — a thing like that is too valuable to lose." His face eased into a smile. "I caught sight of you momentarily in the fog, but you turned and fled. What could I do but follow?"

She felt foolish, well remembering how she had pushed things back into her bag — hurriedly, unseeingly, intent only on getting away from the cold eyes of the hotel clerk and from the man watching nearby. This man, whom she had imagined to be menacing.

"I'm sorry," she said. "I was over-wrought, upset — "

"Because you couldn't get your call to Voshanger? I heard you book it, and naturally it caught my attention."

"Why?"

"Because I live here. Voshanger is my home, and I didn't expect to hear someone calling this isolated spot from a place like the Frankfurterhof."

She was astonished to learn that he belonged here. In Frankfurt he could have been taken for almost any nationality. There were even Scots as dark as he, mostly from the western side with no Norwegian origins. The few words he had spoken to her out of the fog had been in slightly accented English; he could have been Continental, mid-European, English or American, but the one nationality she would never have attributed to him was Scandinavian, a race she had always believed to be predominantly fair.

But looking at him now, he seemed exactly the type of man this rugged landscape would produce. Even his clothes — thick Norwegian sweater, with trousers tucked into hand-stitched calf-length boots of reindeer skin — identified him with his surroundings.

She heard him ordering a Scotch and soda, then he sat down opposite her and continued, "You still haven't explained why you ran away from me."

"To tell you the truth, I was frightened." She finished lamely, "I was tired. My plane had been delayed and I'd been traveling for hours."

"And a strange man staring at you in a strange hotel, then following you through the fog, couldn't have helped. If you doubted my motives, I can't blame you. I took a damn good look at you, as many another man must have done, so I'm not surprised if you thought I was hell-bent on scraping up an acquaintance."

She could hardly admit that she had thought him much more dangerous, that she had found him sinister and threatening. So she said nothing, glad of the intervention of the waiter bringing his Scotch and soda, and then of Sonja Thorsen's arrival. The woman walked in just as the man was saying, "Now let's get started on the proper footing, and introduce ourselves. My name is Kurt Dahl."

Sonja came across to join them, and after that the place began to fill with regular habitués. Sonja introduced her as Mrs. Drummond from England, and

Margaret didn't bother to contradict. Her passport was British and she doubted whether these Norwegians would fully appreciate the demarcation line between England and Scotland. They had probably never even heard of Hadrian's Wall, despite their closely united history.

Many inhabitants of Eastern Scotland, as well as parts of England and Wales, had descended from Viking invaders; similarity in coloring and features abounded. With her Scottish blood from her father's side and Norwegian from her mother's, Margaret looked very much like the people around her, who were themselves a mixture of dark and fair. She didn't look foreign; nor did she feel it.

Before long she was talking about herself, guardedly revealing that she was a professional photographer and letting it be assumed that she was here on a job, but she answered only the most essential questions and offered little voluntary information. Uppermost in her mind was the awareness of why she was here, and of the thing which had brought her. Her quest had to be a lone one, secret and terrifying.

She heard Kurt Dahl's voice beside her.

"If you're here to photograph the *locale*, you must let me show it to you. I'm part-owner of the forests around here. They are my life as well as my business."

Sonja urged Margaret to accept, adding that she couldn't have a better guide than Kurt. The whole thing seemed to be settled for her, making refusal impossible, but now that her earlier fear of the man had gone Margaret found she had no desire to refuse. Through him she might learn much about the neighborhood and its inhabitants, and that was vital to her.

"I want to see more than the forests," she told him. "I want to see the mountains as well. I've had climbing experience."

"Then you must meet Helga. Helga Carlsen. She knows the mountains like the back of her hand. She could make out a route even now."

"Why 'even now'?"

"Because she isn't young any more. In her youth she was a great climber."

Margaret had the fleeting impression that Sonja Thorsen heard the words and kept her glance averted.

"I'll be glad to meet her," Margaret said.

"Shall we make it tomorrow? Ten-thirty? I'll drive you around my forests and then take you to meet Helga." He added something to the effect that Helga Carlsen was his business partner, said good-night, and left.

Later, during a solitary dinner, Margaret reflected again that a meeting with someone well acquainted with the mountains might be a valuable contact. He might even have met her father. So might many of the people she had met this evening, and any one of them could be the sender of the anonymous parcel.

Including Kurt Dahl? The thought was interesting, but unconvincing, for the package must have been airmailed from Voshanger when he was in Frankfurt.

Unless, of course, he had sent it before he went there . . .

Walking back to her chalet, her thoughts were occupied with the question of the anonymous package. Her first step was to trace the sender, but she had no idea how to do so. Briefly she wondered if Sonja Thorsen might be able to help; she seemed a kind, outgoing sort of person, one in whom she might be able to confide when they knew each other better, but developing an acquaintanceship could take time and instinct warned Margaret that she had very little.

Hunting down an unidentifiable person was daunting, but there must be a way. There had to be. Help was what she needed, but help was the last thing she was likely to get.

The path from the hotel was lit intermittently by lamps hung from the trees. Combined with moonlight, the effect was soothing. Margaret's earlier uneasiness was gone; she was calmer than she had felt since leaving Edinburgh. There was serenity in the silence of mountain and forest, and she could see the waters of the fjord, smooth as stretched silk shot through with quiet reflections. The tranquil beauty of this ancient world seemed to reach out and enfold her.

But on opening the door of her chalet

she was startled to find herself faced with darkness. The lights she had left blazing had been extinguished.

She switched them on and knew someone other than a maid had been here. The bedspread had been removed, and the downy Scandinavian quilt, which was the only cover necessary in addition to a sheet, lay like a cocoon in its place. The curtains had been drawn and a bath mat placed on the floor beside the shower cubicle. These were the duties of domestic staff and therefore expected, but the sinister feeling of intrusion was not.

The strange thing was that there was nothing tangible to justify it. Nothing appeared to be out of place, except perhaps the suitcase which she had hastily locked and was now slightly awry on the slatted luggage-stool, but that could have been displaced by the maid going about her duties.

But it could also have been caused by someone trying to open it and thrusting it aside in frustration. It was still locked. Margaret had the key in her bag.

Then she noticed her coat, still where she had flung it upon a chair; previously it had been over the arm with the lining half revealed. She could remember seeing it like that when Olaf the porter plunged the room into a blaze of light, the picture registering with the speed of a camera shutter. Now the coat lay over the back of the chair, the lining hidden.

Why should a maid pick up a coat and throw it down again? If she had been about to place it on a hanger to put in the closet, why change her mind?

And the cigarette pack; after lighting one, Margaret had dropped it onto a coffee table, but now it lay on the floor, its contents scattered. A clumsy maid, or a hurried, impatient searcher? But what could be small enough to hide in a cigarette packet?

Negatives, of course. Negatives barely an inch square.

Margaret's whole body went limp. She leaned against the door and stared around the chalet apprehensively. Had the intruder gone, or was he still lurking in some corner, watching her?

Swiftly, she assessed possible places of concealment. There were only two — the shower cubicle and the clothes closet. But she could see the shower cubicle from where she stood, the glass screen folded back and exposing the naked interior.

That left only the closet. She took a deep breath and, heart thudding, marched across the room and flung open the double doors.

Emptiness stared back at her.

So it was all imagination. It had to be. Imagination coupled with the aftermath of shock which had haunted her from Katmandu to Edinburgh, where it had been doubled and then trebled.

She couldn't expect to recover from experiences like that quickly. She had been lulled into false tranquillity by the peace of this place and by the company of friendly people in a friendly bar, but now her nerves were raw and exposed again.

She began to unpack her overnight bag. The tall chest of drawers served as a dressing table and she carried her toilet articles across to it, pulled open the top drawer to put other items inside; the drawer into which she had thrust the talisman ring.

It was gone.

Margaret ran her hand rapidly through the interior, but found nothing, and at that moment a knock sounded on the door.

The noise startled her so much that she shut the drawer with a slam. She was shaken by the disappearance of the ring, but forced herself to open the door with a semblance of calm.

A man stood within the shadows of the porch. His face could not be seen, but she realized at once that it was not Kurt Dahl, whose figure she knew to be unmistakable even in shadow — or fog.

Without any preliminary, the man said, "I heard you were coming, Mrs. Drummond . . . that you had arrived . . . I urge you to leave again as soon as possible."

The voice was identical with that of the guru.

12

THE sensation was uncanny. It was almost as if she were faced with the man himself, but she pulled herself together and demanded, "Who are you?"

"My name is Brandt. Hans Brandt. I sent your father's things to you."

The voice was still an echo of the guru's and, fleetingly, Margaret recalled his final comment that he would only be able to help her from a distance. Now it seemed otherwise, as if he were here, right on her doorstep.

She groped for the switch of the porch light, but when it shone on the figure of Hans Brandt she saw a man very much shorter than the man in the temple, and much more heavily built, although a resemblance was there, strong and unmistakable.

After a moment she stammered, "Forgive me for staring, but you are very like a man I met in Nepal. He told me about a twin, a thousand miles away — "

"My brother. He told me about you, too."

She opened the door wide and as he entered she asked, "How did he tell you? By thought-transference?"

"Of course. We have no need to write letters."

She indicated a chair and sat down opposite, mentally contrasting him with his brother. Hans Brandt was definitely not the type to live in isolation on a Himalayan slope. The two men could not have been more different, despite the closeness of their relationship.

She asked, "And did your brother sense that I was coming here, and pass the message on, or were you yourself aware of it?"

"I was afraid you might come. I have kept in touch in order to find out."

Brandt seemed a surprising person to meet in this part of the world. He had the same swarthiness of skin which, in the guru, didn't mark him as out of place in that land of strong sun and extreme temperatures, but which made this man seem distinctly at odds with a Scandinavian background. One glance, and you could see he didn't belong.

Margaret said without delay, "Why did you send the parcel anonymously?"

"Because I didn't want you to come here, or to contact me."

"Why not? The fact that you sent my father's things proves you knew him. Naturally I want to hear more about his death from someone who was apparently in touch with him during his last visit. Other things too, such as where he stayed. You must be able to tell me that, otherwise you couldn't have obtained his things."

Brandt made a slight acknowledgment and Margaret continued, "Nor could you have collected them from this hotel because when I telephoned on my way home from Nepal they said he wasn't here. Not that he had left; that he had actually not been staying here. I couldn't believe it. He always stayed at this hotel. There was nowhere else."

"But there was. He stayed with me. The hotel was his usual base, but this time he didn't want his visit known — "

He bit the words off, as if regretting having said so much, and Margaret asked sharply, "Why not?"

"We were — working together."

"In what way?" she asked, surprised.

Brandt seemed unwilling to answer, but finally said, "Your father suspected that some power was at work."

Margaret had an uneasy conviction that he was prepared to say no more, so she pressed, "What sort of power? You must tell me everything, Mr. Brandt. I have a right to know."

"An evil power," he admitted, then closed his lips stubbornly.

Margaret persisted, "Evil in what way?"

The man seemed to give a faint sigh of resignation, then went on, "It was tied up with the revival of a cult — the Cult of Fenris."

Margaret gave a start. One other person had mentioned this cult to her — the man in the temple.

She said slowly, "And my father believed it was active, here in Voshanger?"

Brandt nodded. "He knew that I was here to counteract the forces of evil.

Our motives coincided. Then he got that film."

"So you know what was in it?"

The chalet was silent. Through the open window Margaret heard the waters of the fjord lapping against the shore, and from the hotel the sound of laughter and voices, followed by the shuffling of Brandt's feet on the bare wooden floor as he shifted his position. Then the light was full on his face and she saw in his eyes that he knew the truth.

She said tautly, "It was Erik, wasn't it?"

There was pity in Brandt's eyes as he admitted this, but to Margaret the awareness that her terrible secret was shared with someone was almost a relief. Harboring such knowledge alone had been unbearable and now she resolved never to mention Erik's name to anyone else, otherwise the torture would remain with her. She had loved the man, but to discover an unsuspected and repellent side of his nature made her want to stamp out all memory of him. It was essential to blot him from her mind, or she would never recover her faith in people, or hope to find happiness in the future.

"There are things I must know," she insisted. "First, how my father met his death."

Painfully, Brandt told her that Angus had been killed by an eruption on a nearby mountainside. "A freak electrical eruption which occurs sometimes above Voshanger. Erik went the same way."

"But not at the same time, surely? My father phoned me in Nepal, then booked to call later because I was out. It must have been to tell me about Erik's death, but it was you who made that second call. The line was bad, but I know it was your voice."

Brandt inclined his head in acknowledgment and Margaret continued, "You said my father wanted to break the news to me himself, but that he had to go. Go where?"

"Back to the cleft. The Cleft of Fenris."

"Where Erik had also been killed?"

"Yes."

Brandt went on to explain that the cult met there, and that after the last sabbat

Sorenson must have stayed behind for some reason after the others had left. The only public knowledge came from the press, who reported that a well-known Norwegian climber was missing. Only Angus knew of his whereabouts and the actual cause of his death.

Margaret thought fleetingly of Erik's parents. Let them believe their son was killed while climbing; she would never reveal the truth to them.

"Do you know of any other members of the cult?"

Brandt did not. Many inhabitants knew when the dangerous hour was near; such people would be sure to get away in time.

Margaret asked why he wanted her to leave Voshanger, and he said briefly that because her father had intruded on dangerous ground, the danger could be turned against herself.

Margaret dismissed that. She had no intention of leaving yet, but she realized that she might need this man's help.

"If you need me," he said, reading her thoughts in the same uncanny way of his brother, "come to my church, the

Church of St. Olaf, in the center of the village."

"Your church? Are you working in the same way as your brother in his temple?"

"Yes. We work together."

He went on to explain as gently as he could that her father's body would never be found. Anyone caught in the holocaust was totally annihilated.

Then why, Margaret wondered, had her father risked going back after obtaining the evidence he wanted? Again, Brandt answered her unspoken question.

"Your father had dropped a photograph of you."

She caught her breath as she realized what photograph he was referring to, and why her father had gone in search of it. He had wanted to avoid her being implicated, if it were found.

The knowledge that her father had been killed because of her was the most unbearable thought of all.

13

FIRST thing next morning Margaret reported the theft of the ring. Even to her own ears it sounded unconvincing. Just one article, and of no great intrinsic value — nothing else missing, no locks forced, no signs of burglary. It seemed an unlikely tale and she was grateful to Sonja Thorsen for not appearing skeptical. The woman merely reminded her that the ring had fallen off her finger when she checked in. Perhaps it had fallen off again?

"I didn't wear it again. I put it in my handbag, and later into a drawer. The long top drawer of the chest."

Just a ring? A whole empty drawer for just one ring? No clothes, no jewelry, nothing else at all? Sonja didn't put the questions into words. There was no need.

"It had — sentimental value," Margaret said, acknowledging only to herself that its loss went deeper than that. The ring had belonged to her father; therefore it was part of him. An unlikely part and one she failed to understand, but nevertheless it had been his and she hated the thought of anyone else possessing it.

She was assured that the room would be searched. "Perhaps it will turn up, Mrs. Drummond. You may merely have mislaid it."

Margaret thanked her and turned away, and at that moment Kurt Dahl's powerful figure strode through the main doors and came straight over.

"Good," he said, "you're ready," and swept her out to his Mercedes, his every movement that of a man accustomed to taking control.

He turned left from the hotel, climbing a hill leading away from the village, zooming toward neighboring forests with the fjord dropping away below like a discarded ribbon, and soon they were out of sunlight and into shadow, proceeding along a rough forest track. Light and shade cast a dappled carpet before them and the smell of pines was sharp and pungent. Margaret lifted her face to the sweet air, relishing it.

Kurt spent the morning showing her around. Every now and then her camera-trained eye spotted a spectacular view of an exciting angle. Beneath towering peaks, sky-piercing and white-tipped, forest-lands swept toward the green, glacier-fed waters of the fjord, like enormous cloaks of darker green spread by mighty hands.

"There are legends in these parts, aren't there?" she asked at one point. "Legends of mythical gods?"

"Every country, particularly ancient ones, has its legends and mythical gods."

"But here especially. I understand some gods had cults dedicated to them, like one I was told about quite recently . . . "

Her voice trailed away. He glanced at her and saw that her oval face was tinged with grief, as if she had suddenly recalled some memory from which she had escaped. He wanted to ask what was wrong, but her expression was guarded and withdrawn.

She forced herself to ask for the names of various mountain peaks, but scarcely listened to his replies. Mentioning the Cult of Fenris had reminded her of the guru. Perhaps the unexpected strength she had found, the strength to face up to things and finally to come here, had emanated from him; he had been right when he said that she was going to need courage; right about the Varuna ring also — the ring someone had broken into her chalet to steal.

If an inanimate object such as a ring could have protective powers, a motive was provided for the theft; either to win protection for the thief, or to remove protection from herself. Coupled with Brandt's warning not to linger in these parts, the thought was disturbing.

She realized that Kurt was speaking.

"The person to tell you about the mountains is Helga. She'll give you the name of every peak. I'm only knowledgeable about trees. I went straight from school to the lumber camp, following my father's footsteps."

"Then you didn't inherit the forests?"

"No. Helga took over her brother's share — Fredrick Carlsen was my partner. He had the money and I had the know-how. He bought the forests when they came on the market, and I worked them.

Most of the Norwegian forests are in the east, along the Glommen River; these are the only ones in the mountainous west, and therefore valuable because they have quick access to the Bergen docks."

She asked why Fredrick Carlsen had left the business, and Kurt explained that he had married an American girl and gone to live in the states.

"That annoyed Helga," he added, "but why shouldn't a man marry if he wants to? Fredrick was rich enough to live wherever he wanted, and decent enough to provide for his sister by handing over his share to her, but she wouldn't accept it. Fredrick and I had split the proceeds fifty-fifty, but Helga argued that because their background was a wealthy one and she was comfortable, I should have the greater share because I would now be running the forests single-handed and she would be contributing little."

"She sounds a fair-minded person."

"She's a great person. It took me a long time to capitulate, but finally I did. I've felt under an obligation ever since, so I've reciprocated by taking care of her."

"If you have spent your life in the

183

forests, I imagine you would hate to give them up."

He said decisively, "Anyone who tried to make me would have a fight on his hands, and by God, I enjoy a fight."

He turned right into a private drive.

"And now," he said, "come and meet Helga."

★ ★ ★

Driving up to the house, Kurt recalled Helga's reaction to the news that he was bringing a woman, a stranger, to meet her.

"You'll like her," he had said. "Besides, she's on a job where meeting people like you will be of value. You can talk climbing to your heart's content — she's had some experience, so you won't be talking to an unappreciative audience. You know you'll enjoy that."

Helga Carlsen had not argued or contradicted. That was one of the things Kurt liked about her; her absolute honesty, her ability not only to accept a plain unvarnished truth, but to face up to it when it hurt and not be coy about it when it flattered.

"Her husband — is he with her?"

His hesitation had been barely perceptible. "I don't know anything about her husband, but she's here alone. Why not?"

"What a pity she's married. You haven't been so interested in a woman for years."

"And what makes you think I'm interested now?"

"The fact that you are prepared to take time off from your beloved forests for a woman's sake. You have always kept women separate and apart in your life, conveniently tucked away in Bergen or Stavanger or Oslo. It would be unnatural for a man like you to live without a woman, but the forests have always come first. All right, bring your Mrs. Drummond to see me."

"I'll do that. And by the way, I'm not taking time off from my forests. I'm showing them to her."

He recalled Helga's knowing smile now, as he took Margaret to meet her.

The house was a sprawling lodge overlooking the fjord, with a single-story wing built on, and as he brought the Mercedes to a halt at the apex of the long drive he nodded to the main part of the building and said, "That's my home, and the wing extension is Helga's. Our offices are in between so I have access to them from my place and she from hers. We are neighbors as well as business partners, and it's a satisfactory arrangement — we don't intrude into each other's private lives. Come along — I've no doubt she heard us arrive, so we'll go straight in."

Helga's wing was almost stark in its simplicity, which gave emphasis to magnificent views of forest and fjord through panoramic windows, but Margaret's immediate attention was caught by the uncluttered floors and absence of doors.

One room ran into another in an almost continuous line, and there was an austere, aesthetic touch about the place, a kind of disciplined beauty which suggested that its owner was a person of uncluttered mind and fastidious taste.

There was no one around when Kurt led Margaret into what was obviously the main sitting room, but almost immediately he said, "Helga's coming now."

Margaret was surprised. She could hear nothing, but she had no time to throw Kurt even a questioning glance before a voice said, "Welcome, Mrs. Drummond. It was nice of Kurt to bring you. I have few visitors."

Margaret spun around. The voice came from behind, and the woman's entry had been soundless. The cause was startling. Helga Carlsen's self-propelled wheel chair made no noise whatever.

"Don't look so surprised, my dear. Didn't Kurt tell you I was a cripple? That was thoughtless of you, Kurt."

"It never entered my head," he admitted. "I never think of you as a cripple. You're so damn mobile."

Helga laughed. She was a handsome woman, silver hair immaculately groomed. She was like a magnificent ruin, Margaret thought involuntarily, more splendid in age than in youth; elegant, sophisticated, self-confident enough not merely to overcome the handicap of a wheel chair but even to make it a kind of foil for her personality, the indignity of it merely emphasizing her own supreme dignity and its clumsiness her undeniable grace.

Her good looks were impressive, but as Margaret stepped into a beam of sunlight the outer edges of it touched the woman's face, revealing that it was more than lined, it was ravaged; lines became dark furrows and the eyes, ice-blue and striking, were sunken and underlined with shadows. Even so, they were beautiful, and despite their color there was no coldness in them. They were warm and alive, as if all the remaining strength in that frail, once-lovely body was being consumed to provide the force and intelligence and vitality of those eyes.

"I shun visitors," she admitted, "and but for Kurt's persuasion I would never have invited you. My greatest fear is of pity, and whether or not people are prepared in advance for my crippled state, pity is the one thing I am exposed to most of all."

"How can I pity you, when you don't pity yourself?"

Margaret was rewarded by a warm smile and Helga said, "Let me look at you — really look at you. You know now of my one fear; now learn of my one vanity. I refuse to wear spectacles, except for reading. Once upon a time my eyes were my best feature, and I am still vain enough not to wish to hide them. A little nearer — into the light — ''

Margaret stepped forward, and as Helga stared for a moment Kurt asked, "Is anything wrong?"

"Nothing but surprise," Helga answered in a voice which was light and unconcerned. "I didn't expect an English woman to look so Scandinavian. I call you a woman, but you are really no more than a girl to me."

"My mother was Norwegian."

"Ah — that explains your blonde good looks."

The wheel chair spun away adroitly across the polished floor, and Margaret now understood the absence of rugs and doors. Independence would make this woman resent any form of hindrance or restriction.

Helga continued confidentially, "There is only one thing I have never been able to overcome — the necessity to be lifted in and out of this wheel chair. My spine was injured in a climbing accident years ago. Now I can only climb the mountains in my imagination, but I remember every rock face, every buttress, every groove and traverse. My greatest joy is to drive out in my invalid car and gaze up at the peaks, reliving my past."

Kurt said abruptly, "You shouldn't do it, Helga. I've told you."

Helga continued, as if without interruption, "I suffer the frustration of having to be lifted in and out of the thing, but at least it enables me to get out and about. I can drive to the village, along the fjord road, wherever I please within reason. And, as you can see, I move freely about my house in this chair. I find it galling to have to rely upon a servant to get me in and out of it, but the whole business is treated in the way I want it to be — as a joke. And now — enough of me. Drinks, Kurt." She turned back to Margaret. "Are you Scottish, Mrs. Drummond?"

"It's a good Scottish name," Kurt said.

"I am Scottish, but Drummond, of

course, was my husband's name."

"Was?" Helga repeated.

"We were divorced after two years."

"That is sad, my dear, but you are young enough to be able to look to the future."

"I am sure that you yourself have a great deal to look forward to," Margaret answered quietly.

There was a little silence, and for a moment Margaret wondered if she had said the wrong thing. She glanced at Kurt. His expression was encouraging, and Helga appeared relaxed. They both seemed to approve of her attitude of understanding uncloyed by sentimentality.

Helga answered. "You are right, Mrs. Drummond. I count my blessings. I am a lucky woman — no financial worries, and this home for which I have to thank Kurt. Can you understand a man like Kurt sparing time for friendship with a woman like me?"

"Now that I have met you, yes."

Helga raised her glass.

"I hope you will be my friend, too. Kurt tells me this is your first visit to Norway. How long do you plan to stay?"

"I can take my time. I want to get plenty of pictures."

Kurt put in, "I've told her that you know the mountains like the back of your hand and will be able to advise her where to try for the best shots."

"You've climbed before?" Helga asked Margaret.

"Nearly all my life. In Scotland, Snowdonia, Switzerland."

"But never in Norway? Now that you are here, you must make up for it. I wish I could take you. I hope Kurt also told you that I was once a *good* climber."

"I hinted," said Kurt, his stern face creasing engagingly. He wasn't handsome, like Bruce, but his ugliness could be fascinating.

Margaret sat back, relaxed, feeling unexpectedly at home, listening to Helga's talk about the mountains and the best routes to take.

"I'll map them for you," she offered. "In fact, I still have all my old route charts stacked away somewhere. They were good — or so the man with whom I used to climb often told me. They could be of help to you, now."

For the first time there was a touch of genuine sadness in her voice, a sadness which stopped short of bitterness, but Margaret saw a frown touch Kurt's face and sensed that he wanted to turn the conversation from the course it was about to take.

"Mrs. Drummond was inquiring about our ancient gods," he said, picking the subject at random.

Helga looked surprised. "I didn't think anyone paid any heed to that sort of thing nowadays."

"It's the mountains I'm really interested in," Margaret told her. "As for your ancient gods, I've heard only of one — Fenris the Wolf."

"Son of Loki and Augurboda. A pack of nonsense, of course."

Margaret asked casually, "Wasn't there something about the revival of a cult associated with it?"

"Here? In Voshanger? I don't believe it!" Helga's smile was scornful. "In ancient times it was some sort of religion, like white witchcraft or black magic, but it isn't practiced today! — not that I have ever heard. Have you, Kurt? If anyone should know, it is you. Your life is in the forests. You would be the first to find out if anything peculiar went on there."

"The only thing that goes on in the forests is forestry." For a moment his face was clouded, as if by some worrying picture, then he seemed to thrust it aside as he finished, "And the only thing connected with the name of Fenris is a mountain cleft where some sort of eruption happens occasionally — commonly known as the Rage of Fenris."

At this mention of the cause of her father's death, Margaret's fingers tightened upon her glass, but beneath her distress she heard Helga's sound of amused contempt.

"A perfectly natural phenomenon, as anyone of intelligence knows. That is why climbers avoid that particular spot." She paused, then went on, "I'll mark it on the map as a place to avoid. I've never been near it myself — my accident occurred on the mountains higher up. An avalanche hit me. They are fairly frequent in winter and only experienced climbers go up at such times."

Margaret was shocked. "You could have been killed!"

"Luckily for me, it threw me clear — onto a rock ledge. But my spine was injured and I had to remain there until rescued."

"You were climbing *alone*?"

There was a momentary hush, then Kurt said, "No. Helga was with a climber more experienced than herself. The man abandoned her — left her to die. His name was Angus Buchanan."

14

KURT shut the car door and went around to the driver's seat, wondering why Margaret Drummond was in such a hurry to get away. She had seemed relaxed and at ease, the atmosphere had been friendly, but Helga's invitation to stay to lunch had been politely rejected.

Now Margaret looked pale and withdrawn, but in retrospect he could think of nothing which could have been responsible. For the most part, conversation had been dominated by Helga, talking about the mountains and then becoming dangerously nostalgic. It wasn't often that she lapsed into such a mood; self-pity was unknown to her. For this reason he especially admired her.

The more he pondered over things, the more he failed to understand why Margaret Drummond wanted to leave so suddenly. She had covered it well as she said good-bye to Helga, who urged her to come again and promised to have the route charts ready and waiting. Their leave-taking had been that of two women who liked each other.

During the run down into the village Kurt glanced at Margaret once or twice, troubled by a vague resemblance to someone, so elusive that he was unable to place it. This resemblance had struck him from the moment he first saw her in the Frankfurterhof, and for a long time after she had seized her passport and stumbled back into the taxi he had been unable to forget her. He had pinned his hopes on her turning up here, and although there seemed no reason in the world why she should, there had also seemed no reason in the world why she should not.

A person didn't telephone a hotel hundreds of miles away except to speak to someone, or to make a reservation, and he had persisted with the hope that it was the latter, because at this time of year Voshanger was almost free of visitors.

They came in droves during the winter, *en route* to the snowfields, and sometimes a few came during the summer for fishing .holidays, and during school or college vacations parties came for the climbing, but the skiing season had not arrived yet, and fishing was not at its peak, and school and college vacations weren't due for another month at least, so the hotel was virtually empty and used mainly by local inhabitants.

He had gone over all this in his mind to convince himself that since there were no foreign visitors for her to be telephoning, she must have been making a reservation. At the same time, he had wondered why he couldn't forget her.

If he had not been occupied with problems of his own he might have been tempted to probe deeper, but Helga's reference to his forests now revived these problems, and the anxiety he had brought back with him from Frankfurt stirred again. Perhaps it was a good thing no lunch party had grown out of this visit to Helga. It would have meant small talk, generalities, a three-sided conversation for which he was really in no mood, and it might also have been a strain if Helga's unexpected nostalgia for the past had been allowed to grow.

That was why he had finally laid it

on the line in a tone which closed the discussion, giving the facts about her accident before she herself was tempted to. Helga rarely referred to it, but something seemed to have triggered her off today and she had come dangerously near to revealing her personal feelings.

As he left Margaret at the hotel entrance, Kurt was more than ever convinced that something, somehow, had gone wrong, although her manner couldn't be faulted. She thanked him for taking her to the forests, for the time he had given up, for the introduction to Helga; she omitted nothing, even promising to send him prints of her best shots after she returned home.

"I'd like those," he said. "I'd like to have some really good forest pictures. But I hope you won't be leaving soon?"

"That depends. I may accomplish what I want to accomplish sooner than I expect."

He knew she was talking about her photographic assignment and murmured something about hoping she would not complete it too soon. She smiled, said good-bye and thanks again, and left him.

He watched her walk up the steps into the hotel, but she didn't look back.

Kurt climbed into the Mercedes thoughtfully, and drove home. Normally he went straight into his own part of the house; the entrance was in the front, with Helga's around the side — both, like their lives, self-contained and apart — but the garages were at the back and as he parked the Mercedes he saw Helga's face at the rear window of her sitting room and knew she had been watching for his return.

He could have gone straight to his own quarters but something compelled him to go to hers. He walked straight in and she came to meet him, propelling her chair speedily across the wide bare floor, and as she drew near he saw that her face looked more ravaged than before.

"I didn't know," she said abruptly. "I didn't *know*. I wish I could have stopped you, Kurt."

"Stopped me from what? And what didn't you know?"

"Who she really is. It wasn't until you had blurted out the truth about my accident, that I realized."

"Realized what?" he asked, suppressing

a touch of impatience.

"That Margaret Drummond is Angus Buchanan's daughter. And she didn't say a word. She just left as quickly as she could, but as she walked out of this room I knew who she was."

After a stunned moment he said, "I don't believe it."

"You mean you don't want to. And you don't want to because it can mean only one thing in your eyes; that her freelance assignment is a fake, a trumped-up excuse; that now her father has been killed she is here to carry on where he left off. But you never *knew*, you could never be sure that he was mixed up in all that business."

"It is still going on," he answered grimly, "despite his death. The lawyers in Frankfurt confirmed my worst fears."

"You're a fighter, Kurt. You will win in the end, I'm certain of that."

"I wish *I* could be so sure. Oh yes, I'll fight, but in this day and age the big powers can grind the fighters into the ground. As for Margaret Drummond being Angus Buchanan's daughter, you're wrong — you've got to be wrong."

"I wish I were, but when she stood in that window earlier there was something about her, something which startled and frightened me; a resemblance, a familiarity which I refused to recognize. But when she walked out of this room I was convinced. She holds her head the way he did, has mannerisms of his — and on top of all that she bears a strong resemblance to her mother."

He heard himself saying, "I wouldn't know about that — "

He had never met Nina Buchanan. He had been a child, living in a lumberjack's cottage on the outer rim of the forests, when all that happened, skiing down to the village school in winter and riding two astride on horseback with his brother in the summer. That was the nearest he had come to taking part in the life of Voshanger, but when Helga Carlsen's accident happened everyone for miles around heard about it.

Some of the stories were garbled, but there were still people who believed that Helga's memory had been affected and that Buchanan's own story should have been heeded more. But once the man had told it, he had not stayed to defend himself further. He had married a local girl and taken her to his own country, and given no further thought to the girl he had left to die.

Those who chose to remember what he had said remembered it, but eventually pity for Helga won everyone over. Almost everyone, he corrected. As for Helga's memory, that had been proved sound. No one knew better than he, after the years of their business association, how reliable it was.

He heard Helga say, "If you had paid more attention to her — more objective and less admiring, I mean — you might have noticed the resemblance too."

But he had, although never for a moment had he associated that elusive reminder with Buchanan. Even now, he found it hard to do so — those blonde, almost Scandinavian good looks had not come from the tough sandy-haired Scot whom he had every reason to mistrust.

Buchanan had been blunt-featured, with out-thrust and aggressive chin, square-faced, large-boned; Margaret Drummond was tall but slight, with an oval face and finely-cut features. It wasn't in coloring alone that she differed from her father — if he *were* her father, which he doubted. Unwillingly, Kurt admitted to himself that there was a certain something about her which could indicate the relationship if he looked for it. The truth was that he didn't want to.

15

ON entering the hotel after Kurt had dropped her, Margaret pulled up sharply when she saw Bruce, then walked slowly across to him. He waited, because it pleased him. Concerned for her as he was, he wasn't going to rush to meet her. He had checked in half an hour ago, glancing at earlier entries as he did so. He couldn't miss hers; it was on the line above. He had promptly inquired for her, to be told by a middle-aged woman that Mrs. Drummond had gone out.

He had waited none too patiently, sitting here admiring the view of the forests and scanning the vast stretches covered by them. Voshanger was situated in a sprawling valley, with endless reaches of land and water. The man who owned those forests was on to a good thing.

He had also been mentally rehearsing all the things he was going to say to Margaret when they met, but now he was face to face with her he couldn't say any of them. He was only conscious of relief because he had found her. He rose as she approached, and she said, "I suppose you are angry."

"I was. Not any more."

"How did you find me?"

"I'll tell you later. You look tired. Where have you been?"

She couldn't tell him because a feeling of being intruded upon was as great as her surprise. She didn't like being supervised, or questioned, and she didn't want him tailing her. She didn't want anyone tailing her. So she made an evasive answer about having been for a walk, and mercifully he let it go at that, although somehow she felt he didn't quite believe her.

She could see curiosity in his eyes and a long line of questions waiting to be asked, but she wasn't ready to tell him about Hans Brandt, or Helga Carlsen, or why she was feeling so shaken after meeting the woman. If Bruce put her constraint down to tiredness, so much the better.

He said gently, "I was anxious about

you and had to come. We'll talk over lunch, shall we?"

She agreed unwillingly, covering it with a smile, but he had an uncomfortable feeling that she was not pleased to see him. He had known she would be surprised; what he had not expected was resentment. Most women were gratified when a man showed concern for them, especially if it brought him hot-foot in pursuit, but the expression upon Margaret's face, the polite smile coupled with a suggestion of stubbornness about the mouth, hinted otherwise. It was not the kind of reception he had expected, and it hurt.

After he had ordered, he said with a touch of reproof, "I take it you're not particularly glad to see me."

"I'm sorry. I just wanted to be left alone. I still want to be." His answering silence made her feel ashamed, and she hurried on, "You're kind, but I've got to get over things by myself, in my own way."

He decided she was still overwrought. "Why did you follow me, Bruce?"

"I've told you — I was anxious. Why

did you leave so suddenly, and without letting me know? We spoke on the phone the night before you left. I had tried earlier in the evening, but got no reply. I suppose you had gone for a walk?"

She remembered the telephone ringing as she left her flat, and how she had refused to go back because of her impatience to get to her father's laboratory. She colored slightly, and Bruce took it as a gratifying sign of guilt, the kind a child shows when caught in some misdemeanor. She knew he interpreted it in that way, and was glad but irritated. She wasn't a child, she was a woman, and what she was feeling was a very adult alarm in case he probed deeper and found out where she had gone, and why. She was not prepared to tell him that yet.

Hostility rose in her. "What is this?" she demanded. "An inquisition? Now tell me why you have really come."

"To take you back to Edinburgh and safety."

"What is unsafe about this place?"

"Isn't it sufficient that both your father and the man you were presumably going to marry have died terrible deaths here?"

"Accidents."

"*You* could meet with an accident too, going up these mountains alone. And don't tell me you're not planning to. Climbers can never keep away from them."

"I've been taught to be careful."

"So was your father. He was an expert. One of *the* experts."

"He was killed by an electrical storm. Not even the most expert climber could escape that, but I can because I've been warned of the danger spot."

"By whom?"

"Local people."

"Then surely Angus must have known, too? Come, Margaret, be reasonable. If this place had been safe for you to visit, your father wouldn't have kept you away from it all these years."

She hardly heard what he said, because suddenly she found herself comparing him with Kurt Dahl. The two men could not have been more different. Despite Bruce's decisiveness, his air of authority, and his kindness and concern for her, the Norwegian was the more compelling.

She became aware that Bruce was saying something about an inquest.

"One will have to be held on both deaths. I know Professor Sorenson and his wife have come over for their son's, and are already at their house outside Bergen. I will attend your father's. You can leave all the formalities to me, Margaret. Angus was my business partner, remember, so I must definitely establish his death. After that, I am taking you home."

★ ★ ★

Kurt found Sonja Thorsen alone in her office. This was what he had hoped for. He was anxious to obtain proof of Margaret Drummond's relationship with Angus Buchanan, if such a relationship existed.

Helga's conclusions might well be right, but a certain physical resemblance was not enough to go on, nor was Helga's interpretation of Margaret's behavior at her house. A woman who had suffered as Helga had suffered could be excused for allowing painful reminders to enlarge into fancy.

210

In Sonja Thorsen he saw a possible source of help, but putting the question was difficult. He knew her to be reserved, and suspected that she was also sensitive; reserved people usually were.

He liked Sonja, although circumstances had placed them on opposite sides of the camp long ago. He also pitied her although he was careful never to reveal it, knowing that pity, to a woman as proud as she, would be an insult.

She was sitting at her desk when he opened the office door and walked in. She smiled faintly, and he interpreted the smile correctly. *A man like you, Kurt Dahl, would never dream of knocking* . . . And she was right. He was not the sort of man to tap humbly on doors.

Then he saw inquiry in her eyes. She was waiting for him to explain his visit. Not for the first time, he wished that he knew her better. Sonja Thorsen was the sort of woman most men wanted to know, whatever her age. He judged her to be about forty, the kind of woman who would carry her good looks through the years because they were based more on character and expression than on superficial appearance.

Now she swiveled around in her office chair, still looking at him, still waiting, still with that quizzical expression upon her face which said, *You came to me — so go ahead.*

He went ahead, coming to the point with characteristic bluntness.

"I want to talk to you about Mrs. Drummond."

She stiffened imperceptibly and the quizzical glance became watchful, alert. She never discussed guests with anyone, as he should well know. This was what her eyes said, but behind the expression lay a great deal more — even, he felt, a touch of apprehension.

Again his pity for her stirred. She was a woman who had grown accustomed to wearing a mask and assumed it automatically whenever necessary.

She assumed it now. He saw her defenses go up, the customary shield, and he thought what a waste it was that a woman such as she had never married. Many a man had wanted her, and many a man still would.

He burst out suddenly, "Why, in the

name of heaven, can't you and I be friends?"

"You know why," she answered calmly. "We both know why. And that is the reason for stopping this conversation."

"It hasn't even begun, and I won't be got rid of, Sonja, because this is important to me. What do you know about Margaret Drummond?"

"Why should I know anything about hotel guests, providing they are not criminals?"

There were degrees of crookedness, he thought, but merely asked whether she was certain that Margaret Drummond actually was a travel photographer on an assignment.

Sonja studied him for a moment, then answered evasively, "You took her to see the forests. What was your impression? Didn't she take her camera with her?"

"Of course."

"Well, then?"

He pointed out that shots of the vicinity could be used for other purposes, but when Sonja demanded to know exactly what purposes he refused to be drawn. There were things which he intended to keep to himself until the appropriate time. Vital things. The trip to Frankfurt had been well worthwhile.

"Does she remind you of anyone?" he asked without warning.

"Should she?"

"Helga thinks so."

"Then ask Helga."

He thought admiringly that Sonja was clever; she had learned the art of fencing long ago. Living as she lived, in the heart of a community, and in a fairly public capacity, this had become necessary for self-protection.

He tried again. "Has it occurred to you that Margaret Drummond could have links with this place?"

"It has not occurred to me," Sonja replied coolly, "because she has never been here before. Apart from the fact that has told me this, a person who is a complete stranger to a place betrays it in a hundred different ways, including total unfamiliarity with the layout. Mrs. Drummond doesn't even know her way around the village yet."

When he pointed out that it seemed odd for a young Scotswoman to come here alone, trying to find out all she could about the region, Sonja's clear gray eyes merely looked back at him frankly. They were beautiful eyes and always would be, even in old age. Again he thought what a waste it had been for such a woman to live her life as she had done.

He heard her answering negligently that Mrs. Drummond's job seemed sufficient explanation. "But if you want a more detailed one, why don't you ask her yourself, Kurt?"

"I intend to. I hoped to get some proof before I did so."

"I can offer you none."

She turned back to her desk, but although she appeared to continue with her work he knew well enough that it was pretense. She was turning papers unseeingly, reading them without taking in their contents, writing meaninglessly on a memo-pad.

He was sorry he had come, but the need and compulsion had been strong. The last thing he wanted to do was hurt or embarrass this woman. He stood there, wondering how to break down the barrier between them, but not for the sake of probing into her personal affairs. As with himself, her life was her own, her opinions and beliefs her own, and he had no desire to encroach upon either.

He said gently, "Circumstances which have prevailed for years should not have prevented friendship between us."

She raised her head, half turned, and he saw her eyes quickly fill with tears. Then she turned away again and stared unseeingly through the window into the garden beyond.

His glance followed.

The hotel was built on three wings around a central quadrangle which formed a paved terrace above the garden, and the office looked straight onto it. He could see the two adjoining wings, with the hotel doors leading from the central one. The window also commanded a fine view of the garden and fjord, of the path leading toward the chalets and another to the boat jetty, but he saw none of this because his glance was suddenly arrested by a couple emerging from the main doors onto the terrace.

He took a sharp breath. The light

from the clear, northern skies touched the woman's blonde head and the dark one of her male companion. He watched them descend the steps leading down into the garden, then demanded harshly, "Is that man staying here?"

"Yes."

"When did he arrive?"

"Today."

"What is his name?"

Sonja swiveled around in surprise. She wondered why Kurt was so curious, and said so.

He answered desperately, "I *have* to be. Trust me — and tell me his name."

She gave a helpless, bewildered shrug. He would find out soon enough anyway. Guests at the hotel became known very quickly.

"His name is Matheson," she said.

Kurt demanded swiftly, "Bruce Matheson — from Edinburgh?"

"Why, yes — "

Kurt's mouth tightened. He thought as much. All the questioning in the world could not have offered him such conclusive proof as this.

Margaret slept badly that night, disturbed by dreams of Angus appearing and disappearing on some unknown mountain while she stood on the other side of a cleft, straining to reach him. But the gulf could not be bridged; the more she strove to span it the wider it became, until eventually he was lost from view and in place of the cleft was a roaring avalanche with Helga's twisted body struggling against it.

She had wakened with a feeling of panic and a chill down her spine, unable to reorientate herself, aware only that the nightmare about Helga had gone but that she was still in darkness, searching for her father. Then consciousness returned fully, bringing with it a sense of devastating loss and the knowledge that she was never to see him again.

Grief, which she kept under control by day, now took over, and she surrendered to it with the abandonment of one who had learned to conceal her innermost feelings from the eyes of the world.

Eventually fatigue overcame her. She

was drawn into a deeper darkness, but not into oblivion, for once more she was reaching out to her father across a gulf, calling him back, her voice a dying echo in eternal silence. Then suddenly she wakened with a terrifying jolt, immediately conscious.

He had gone. He had been killed. And but for her it would never have happened.

Daylight pierced the shutters, slicing the room like prison bars, and suddenly the chalet seemed like a cell from which she had to escape. She rose immediately, showered, toweled vigorously, brushed her long hair, tied it back, forgot about make-up and stepped out into the early morning air. It was sharp and clear, the smell of pines from the forests coming to her on the wind, reminiscent of Scotland and home.

Breakfast held no appeal. She needed exercise, fresh air, time in which to banish the lingering aftermath of nightmare; time to harness self-control before facing people again. This was what Angus would expect her to do.

'Don't look back over your shoulder.

You've got to go forward, and the going will be easier if you face up to it.'

It seemed as if he were helping her now, the words echoing in her mind as she walked down to the fjord. To reach the shore she had to take a path skirting the approach to the hotel, and as she did so she glanced toward it unseeingly. The place was stirring; shutters were being opened; at one window a woman's face appeared, shadowy beyond the dim pane, lingering as Margaret passed. She paid no heed and went on.

At the water's edge she stepped out briskly. Shingly patches of beach were linked by rough paths, and here and there rocks stretched from the fjord to the road above, where already laborers were cycling or trudging to work and occasional cars went roaring by. Margaret saw a school bus, packed with children, threading its way through the early morning traffic. She watched for a moment, then turned toward the fjord.

Down here the world was deserted, except for fishermen launching their boats for the deeper stretches where salmon lurked. Sometimes, when the North Sea was wild, shoals of porpoise sought refuge within the fjords, leaping and diving like some marine ballet until the water was whipped into a frenzy and the fishermen were forced to escape to quieter stretches, but now the fjord was as smooth as glass, the wake of the boats scarcely ruffling the surface.

Margaret sat down upon a rock to watch their departure, observing the prows of their craft which still had a Viking touch about them. She watched until they reached the center of the fjord and began to cast their nets. It was a scene as old as time, with the quietness of time, and the serenity of it calmed her. The lingering traces of her nightmare receded.

But still she had no desire to go back to the hotel. The fishermen were now sitting like hunched statues in their boats, waiting with the patience of fishermen the world over, then moving on quietly, dragging their nets.

She watched for a while, then let her glance roam to the opposite shore where fir-clad slopes rose sheer from the water and, high above, snow-capped peaks plunged into the sky. Through the density of forest and rock, silver cascades poured down from limitless heights, emptying the mineral content of glaciers into the fjord and so imparting its vivid emerald color.

Those slopes formed part of Kurt Dahl's forests — and there were more in the valley beyond a far curve in the fjord, where the earth spread out for mile after mile, dense with the tall trees which he planted, nurtured, and replenished year after year, life cycle following life cycle.

High upon the sheer cliffs on the opposite shore, toy houses seemed to perch precariously. Kurt had driven her up a zig-zag trail yesterday, showing them to her. They were loggers' homes, each with its small patch of cultivated earth reclaimed from the mountainside, many with clotheslines of long grass hung out to dry — fodder to be stored against the winter for the goats which supplied the family milk.

Higher still, reindeer stalked, to be hunted and killed and hung for winter food, and their skins utilized for boots and coats. It was a wild, tough world, for all its beauty. Only down here, in Voshanger and similar fjord townships, had the comforts of life become essentials.

Margaret rose. It was time to face people again, and she was ready to do so. She was even aware of the pangs of hunger and, as she reached the hotel's landing stage and the path leading up from it, she was also aware of the need to tidy her wind-blown hair. She went back to her chalet, but as she reached the door she heard movements from within. The maid was about her duties early. Margaret pushed open the unlatched door, and stepped inside.

But it wasn't a maid. It was Sonja Thorsen.

She was standing by the chest of drawers, with the top one open and the Varuna ring in her hand.

16

MARGARET closed the door and they looked at each other in silence. Then Sonja held out the ring.

"I was putting it back."

Her voice was taut, strained, rigidly controlled; the voice of a woman who had been holding herself in check for a long time.

When Margaret stared at her, unable to speak, Sonja plunged on desperately, "Don't you understand? *I took*. But I — couldn't keep it — "

The hand extending the ring was trembling and the other, holding on to the drawer, clutched so tightly that the knuckles showed white.

Margaret said gently, "Sit down, Sonja — "

The woman didn't seem to hear. She took a deep, uncertain breath and burst out, "I'm glad you know. Hiding the truth isn't — easy."

Margaret urged her into a chair and as she did so Sonja seized her hand and pressed the ring into it.

"Forgive me," she pleaded.

Margaret was touched. A trinket, a bauble, a valueless ring with some superstition attached to it — what sort of a theft was that, and why should a woman who was materially comfortable stoop to it? The act seemed so meaningless that it was pathetic.

Margaret dropped the ring into her pocket.

"There's no need to be frightened or worried," she said. "I don't know why you took the ring unless it attracted you when I dropped it. I saw you studying it as you gave it back to me, but somehow I don't think you imagined it had any intrinsic value. It hasn't, of course. Anyway, you brought it back, so let's forget the whole thing." She added impulsively, "Do you know, the ring is believed to have protective powers?"

Sonja nodded.

"Is that why you took it?"

"Of course not." Derision touched the woman's mouth, and Margaret immediately asked how she had known about the superstition.

"Your father told me."

Margaret was startled. "You knew my father?"

"I knew him well," Sonja answered gently. "That was my reason for taking the ring. I have nothing of his. Nothing to remember him by."

In the silence which followed, Margaret realized that she was confronted with something about which she had never known. The truth was in the woman's face and for a moment Margaret could not speak. The fact that her father had had a mistress did not shock her; it was natural that there should have been women in the life of such a man, but somehow she had never suspected the existence of one particular woman whom he had traveled abroad to visit regularly.

If this was his reason for never taking his daughter along with him Margaret was not hurt, merely puzzled. Between two people who respected each other's right to live his life, such a reason was unncessary.

Sonja was plainly wanting to leave.

Margaret begged her to remain, but when she did so Margaret found herself at a loss for words. She could only stare at the woman, seeing her as one who had apparently played an intimate part in her father's life, but at length she managed to ask, "How long did you know him?"

"We met shortly after I became manageress here. He was staying in the hotel. It was the first time he had been in Voshanger for many years, he told me."

"So you didn't know my mother?"

"No, but Angus told me all about her. As soon as they met, he fell in love with her and she with him. It was as simple as that. He took her back to Scotland, and married her."

Sonja went on to say that she herself had fallen in love with him in the same way — an instant awareness which deepened rapidly, until it was not only a permanent part of her life, but the most essential. No other man interested her after that, and she now doubted whether any man would be able to fill the gap which Angus had left.

Margaret fell silent, too moved to

227

speak. She pitied Sonja, but at the same time envied her. To love a man so completely that total trust went with it, and life became empty without him, was something every woman hoped to experience. Somewhere in her affair with Erik that total trust had been lacking. There was no other explanation for her hesitation about marrying him, although her emotional involvement had blinded her to the fact.

She became aware that Sonja was still talking.

"It wasn't until Angus paid his second visit here that he began to feel as I did. He returned very soon and I couldn't hide my delight, especially when I learned that he had been unable to forget me."

Unthinking, Margaret reached toward the coffee table for cigarettes. Sonja's glance followed, and she said apologetically, "I sent those flying when I searched the chalet. I'm sorry I didn't wait to pick them up, but I had to get away quickly — "

Margaret shrugged and held out the package. Over the flame of the lighter she looked at the woman sympathetically, but still with a touch of envy for although Sonja Thorsen's life had apparently been empty, it had at least been filled with the kind of dedicated devotion which, in the deep recesses of her heart, Margaret wanted to experience and had not yet found.

Perhaps she never would. The thought of Bruce's solicitude warmed her — but was that enough?

"There is something else I want to talk about," she said suddenly. "Helga Carlsen's accident."

"So you've heard about that? I was afraid you might." Sonja's gray eyes sparked angrily. "It cannot possibly be true, as everyone who really knew your father must believe."

"Did he ever discuss it with you?"

"Once, but after telling me his version he never referred to it again. It happened just after he met Nina, and shortly before he took her away from here." Sonja's glance became troubled. "When Kurt suggested you should meet Helga, I was afraid you might hear the whole tragic story. Her version. I mean."

"But I didn't. She said nothing. It

was Kurt who mentioned it. He said my father was responsible for her being crippled, that he abandoned her during an avalanche, to save himself." Margaret's voice shook, but she added, "Of course, he had no idea that Angus Buchanan was my father. I'm sure he would never have mentioned it, otherwise."

Knowing nothing of Kurt's visit to Sonja's office, or of his questions regarding her identity and of Sonja's worried speculation as to the reason, Margaret failed to understand the look of anxiety which came into the woman's eyes now, but a moment later it had gone and she was saying, "Unfortunately, that is what they believe — Kurt and Helga. It has been a barrier between us for years."

"But *why* should they believe it?"

"Because that is the way she remembers it." Sonja moved restlessly, crossing to the window and back again. "That is her version, Margaret."

"And — my father's?"

"He was climbing with Helga, and they *were* caught in an avalanche. It was sudden, and short. He managed to get hold of her and save her, but before they could escape another avalanche hit them, more violent than the first. He battled through it and thrust her onto a ledge of rock above the danger mark, but he himself was swept away."

Margaret made an instinctive gesture of shock and Sonja hurried on, "When he escaped and the avalanche subsided, he climbed back in search of Helga, only to find she had been picked up by a rescue party."

"Surely she knew this?"

"You know what she believes, but it can only be due to the fact that her injuries caused hallucination or loss of memory." Sonja sighed. "Unhappily, it is too late to clear that up now, but those of us who believed in your father will go on believing in him."

"But Kurt Dahl isn't one of them," Margaret said thoughtfully.

"Are you surprised? He never really knew Angus, but he did, and does, know Helga. Her bravery won many people over, particularly in view of the fact that she has never harbored bitterness. Even when Angus returned after all those years she met him with friendliness, as if nothing had happened. One can't help but admire her."

Sonja stubbed out her cigarette and ran a tired hand through her hair. It was time to let her go.

Margaret moved to the door. "Will you walk up to the hotel with me?" she asked. "I haven't breakfasted yet."

They walked out into the morning sunshine together, both aware that there were many things still unsaid. It was Margaret who turned to them.

"So you have known my identity ever since I arrived?"

"Almost. You have characteristics which are very reminiscent of your father. Gestures, mannerisms, the way you turn your head, the shape of your forehead. Other things; inevitable things. I noticed them when you walked into the hotel. Everything about him, you see, was familiar and dear to me."

Margaret commented that physical resemblance alone could not have betrayed her identity — the ring must have done that.

"Not entirely. It just happened to be identical with one Angus had shown me, and it gave me a shock when you dropped it, but other people might own similar rings. Then you signed the register, and I saw your passport bearing your place and date of birth. Coupled with your address in the hotel register, an Edinburgh address, everything pointed to your identity, but I was still unsure. Naturally, I was anxious to know."

"Because of your relationship with my father?"

"Of course. If you were actually his daughter, you would be a link with him, and he wouldn't be so entirely lost to me. We gave each other great happiness. I had waited for it for a long time and so, in some ways, had he." Grief was in the woman's voice as she finished, "And now he has gone, and no man can ever take his place."

Impulsively, Margaret took the ring from her pocket.

"Keep this, Sonja. I want you to have it."

Tears filled Sonja's eyes and her lips moved soundlessly.

"You must have loved him very deeply," Margaret said, and it was she who now put the ring into the palm of Sonja's hand and closed the fingers over it.

In a few minutes they would be at the end of the path and in full view of the hotel. Sonja halted, reluctant to go further. From the moment she had found the ring in Margaret's drawer the impulse to touch it, to hold in her hand something which had belonged to Angus, had been too strong to overcome, and suddenly it was essential to explain just why and how she had gone to Margaret's chalet that night.

"When I passed the door of the bar and saw you sitting there, I slipped down, knowing the coast was clear. I was almost, but not quite, certain you were Angus's daughter, but the thing which finally convinced me was the camera case. I noticed it when you registered. It was one of your father's, wasn't it?"

Margaret admitted that it was, and Sonja went on to explain that she had found it on the chair beneath Margaret's coat.

"The moment I saw the rubbing on the strap I was certain. I used to go out with Angus when he was photographing; sometimes I carried the lighter gear, and this camera was one — with his initials, small and unobtrusive, the way he marked all his equipment. What impulse made me open the drawer, I don't know. It was as if something compelled me, just as it compelled me to keep what I found inside."

Margaret said warmly, "I wish you had married him. Why didn't you?"

"I was afraid to. Our relationship was a good one, a happy one, but sometimes I wondered whether it was perhaps no more than consolation for him, and that if we married it would descend to that level. I didn't want to be a kind of substitute wife who couldn't revive the particular kind of happiness he knew with Nina."

She cast a quick glance at Margaret, and added, "Besides, I didn't want anything to come between us, and you might not have taken to me. How were we to know how you would react?"

"My father should have known me better. He should have known that nothing he did would antagonize me."

"And yet a rift had grown between you. Oh, he didn't tell me in so many words — I knew intuitively. There was sadness in his voice when he talked of you recently, a different sadness from when your marriage broke up."

"So you knew about that — "

"Angus told me at the time. He was worried about you, unsure how you were going to get over it, what sort of an effect it was going to have on you. I think he was afraid you might get emotionally involved with another wrong man solely because you were unhappy."

So Sonja knew nothing about Erik. Margaret was grateful to her father for keeping that knowledge to himself. She was also sure that he had kept from this woman all knowledge of the Cult of Fenris.

Margaret plucked idly at an overhanging tree, and asked, "Do you know anything about my mother's death?"

Sonja admitted that Angus had never said much about it. "All I know is that she died of an illness which could never be diagnosed. I know little more than that."

Sonja moved on, but Margaret remained still, so that the older woman was forced to look back.

"A little more," Margaret said pleadingly, "could be so much more than I know myself."

Reluctantly, Sonja told her that, according to her father, Nina had gradually lost the will to live, and no one knew why. She had loved her husband and child, but even that love had not sparked her desire to live. Doctors were baffled and unable to help, although everything was tried.

"Angus said she seemed to surrender to something stronger than herself, something she was powerless to fight, and slowly wasted away. It was almost as if she were — haunted. Or doomed."

A cloud passed across the sun and for a moment the wind was chill. Margaret shivered, feeling as if an icy finger had touched her heart.

Sonja slipped an arm about her shoulders, urging her forward, and Margaret warmed to the comfort the woman offered. She was more affected by this meeting than she had realized at

237

first, but now she not only felt that she had discovered a chapter in her father's life, about which she had known nothing, but was aware of a feeling of kinship with the woman whom he had loved during the latter years of his life.

"Did you see him on his last visit?" she asked as they turned toward the hotel steps.

Sonja confessed that she had not, and that it was the first time he had not stayed with her, nor let her know of his coming. She admitted, in sudden anguish, that she had been hurt by his silence.

"*Why* didn't he want to be with me?" she cried. "I only learned of his visit when the press reports of his death appeared!"

Margaret's heart went out to her, and she answered gently, "I can guess why he didn't get in touch with you, Sonja. Because he wouldn't run the risk of involving you in something which could shock and perhaps injure you. That is all I can tell you now, but later I will tell you more — also where he stayed."

They had reached the hotel entrance.

Sonja was pushing open one of the double doors, but for a moment she paused and looked back at Margaret in a puzzled sort of way.

"But I can guess where he stayed," she said. "It must have been at his house."

Margaret stopped short.

"His *house*? My father had a *house* — here in *Voshanger*?"

17

AT the best of times it would be impossible to do justice to the enormous meal which the Norwegians called breakfast, and this morning the *smorrebrod* of cooked meats, cheeses, fish, stewed fruits, salads, hot bread, rolls and an endless variety of jams, jellies and pickles, all stacked upon a table in the center of the room for self-service, failed to tempt Margaret at all.

She contented herself with the routine boiled egg, toast and coffee which were brought automatically to her table as a preliminary to the main part of the meal, along with the jug of cold milk which completed the menu at the start of a day.

She pushed the jug of milk aside, poured a cup of strong black coffee, and let her mind dwell on this latest piece of news. She was so astonished to learn that her father had owned a house in Voshanger that she ate her food unheedingly, aware only of an intense curiosity which Sonja had awakened but failed to satisfy. Further questions had been forestalled by a summons from the office and the woman had departed, the demands of work claiming her.

But Margaret had to know more about this house of her father's and as she sipped the coffee her thoughts switched to Hans Brandt. He had made no mention of the house, a fact which doubled her curiosity. It seemed to her that the man must undoubtedly know about it.

Everything seemed to come back to Brandt, and in recollection she felt that he had told her little, yielding no more than essential facts. By implication it had appeared that he was Angus's only friend in Voshanger, but all the time he must have known about Sonja Thorsen. He might have thought it tactful not to refer to their relationship, but Margaret wished she had known about it long ago.

She buttered a piece of toast mechanically, her mind reverting to the house. She had an overwhelming desire to visit it, and to do that she must learn of its exact location.

She decided to call on Brandt immediately. Not only had he been her father's friend, but as pastor of the local church he would be familiar with every house in the vicinity and could therefore not plead ignorance.

She left her half-touched breakfast and hurried down to her chalet to collect her coat, but as she approached the door she stood still abruptly. A man was standing there. He had the air of one who had been waiting for some time and had no intention of giving up.

It was Kurt Dahl. He looked at her unsmilingly and in that instant he seemed as menacing as on the night of the fog.

"I was waiting for you," he said without greeting. "It's time we had a talk."

Margaret walked up the steps, unlocked the door of the chalet, and asked casually, "About what?" but beneath her assumed indifference she felt a touch of alarm. This was not the man who had driven her through the forests. He had been friendly then, easy to talk to, likable. Now he was a stranger again, and his frown was forbidding.

She left the door open for him and as

he followed her inside he said, "What else could we talk about but your reason for coming to Voshanger?"

She picked up her camera and he glanced at it with amusement. "There's no need to keep up *that* pretense, Mrs. Drummond. You're not here on any photographic assignment."

She felt the deep flush which rose to her face and was as annoyed by that as she was by him, but she put the camera down again.

"I don't know what you are talking about," she replied, and the trite words annoyed her even more.

"Then let me make it plainer."

There was a steely note in his voice and a steely touch in his grasp as he took hold of her and turned her to face a side window through which could be glimpsed a distant view of the forests.

Standing behind her, he pointed over her shoulder and said grimly, "*There. There*, is your reason for coming to Voshanger. That whole area — hundreds of acres, miles of trees which are not only beautiful but valuable. And that is how I intend them to remain. Understand?"

She spun around and stared at him. "No. I don't understand. Why shouldn't your forests remain as they are?"

Impatiently, he told her to stop pretending, and asked if she honestly thought that he didn't realize now why she had been eager to see his forests and to photograph the terrain.

He stood squarely before her, forceful, demanding. A spate of questions leaped into her mind, but she thrust them back. If, for some unknown reason, he wanted to confuse or frighten her, she was determined not to give him that satisfaction. She decided to ignore him instead.

But as she walked past him he caught hold of her arm and stated calmly that he knew she was here to carry on where her father had left off.

Her head jerked up in surprise.

"My father? You knew my father — and why he was here?"

"I was acquainted with him, no more than that, but I guessed what he was up to the night I saw him coming out of the foothills, carrying his camera. He even had the nerve to signal for a lift!

Needless to say, I drove on."

Margaret sat down slowly. If this man knew what her father had been photographing, then he knew all about the Cult of Fenris, despite his pretense of ignorance.

She looked at him carefully, not wanting to reveal her suspicion but wondering if it were possible that he was one of the unknown members of the Cult, one of those who knew when the dangerous hour was near and so had escaped in time. Why else had he been on that particular stretch of road at that particular moment?

The thought dismayed her so much that she was unaware that he was speaking again until his words slowly began to register, then dismay gave way to confusion.

" . . . I guessed he must have been out with that camera of his long before the light failed. There would be no point in taking reconnaissance pictures in the dark."

"Reconnaissance?" Margaret echoed, puzzled. She now had even less idea of what he was talking about, and said so.

Kurt moved impatiently, again insisting that pretense would get her nowhere.

"I know you are Angus Buchanan's daughter, and I know Bruce Matheson was his partner. I was suspicious even before I went to Frankfurt to see the lawyers handling the take-over — and now I know why you were there too."

She ran a bewildered hand through her hair as she explained that her flight from Delhi to London had been grounded for a few hours at Frankfurt, and that there had been no other reason for her being in that city.

Kurt looked at her doubtfully. For a moment she felt that he wanted to believe her, but refused to.

She shrugged and turned away. "I know nothing about any take-over," she said, "but I'm quite sure my father wasn't involved in anything like that. Why should he be? He was a mountaineer and photographer. Why should he want to get hold of anyone's forests?"

"For the same reason as his partner. I learned a lot in Frankfurt. A German-U.S. combine was behind the setup, the lawyers said, but I found out that the headquarters aren't in Frankfurt, or in America. They are in Edinburgh; the central office of a vast concern headed by Bruce Matheson."

"My father and he were partners in a photographic business, nothing else."

"Then why was your father here so secretly? I know it was he whom I saw the night before I left for Frankfurt. I recognized him at once. I was driving along the fjord road on my way back from Bergen — I'd been settling the dispatch of a new consignment of timber before taking off the next morning. Angus Buchanan had never kept his visits secret before, so this time there must have been good reason."

"There was," she burst out, "but not what you think!"

"Then tell me," Kurt challenged quietly. When she made no answer he shrugged. "I thought as much — you are afraid to admit the truth because he was here on the same job as yourself; learning all about the locality, photographing it *and*, I expect, meeting local people who are anxious for the take-over to succeed."

The injustice so outraged her that she protested furiously, "You are ready to believe the worst of my father because you already believe that dreadful story about him being responsible for crippling Helga Carlsen, but he would have been incapable of such a thing. I knew him; you didn't. But even you must be aware that a man in his line of work could have no possible reason for wanting to own forest-lands."

"I'll give you the reason." The icy note was back in Kurt's voice. "To tycoons like Matheson, land given over to the mere cultivation of trees is a whole world of potential wealth being wasted. Get rid of the trees and install a vast hydroelectric plant, sweep away the countryside, desecrate the valley and industrialize it — *that* is what should be done, in his opinion. And, no doubt, in your father's. Why should he work with Matheson on one project alone?"

For a moment Margaret was too stunned to speak, then she was blurting out wildly that she didn't believe a word of it, that it was lies, all lies, but Kurt pointed out remorselessly that there was power on tap in the vast waters of the fjord, enough power to add millions a year to the tycoon's till.

"So why should a mere forester be allowed to stand in the way?" he finished bitterly. "But let me tell you this, Mrs. Drummond — I'll fight to the last ditch, even if it takes every penny I have."

He made an expressive movement. There was disgust and anger in it. Then he looked hard at her and said, "What sort of a woman are you, coming here the moment your father is killed, joining up with his partner, determined not to let even his death interfere with greed and ambition?"

She was shaking uncontrollably, but as he walked to the door she flung after him, "My father was here for a different reason, for a reason you know nothing about! Ask Hans Brandt. My father was staying with him."

Kurt gave an abrupt laugh.

"Hiding?" he taunted. "So that no one should see him at the hotel, or know he was anywhere around? Whatever excuse he gave to Brandt, I'm quite sure it was untrue. The whole thing has been an underground attack from the start. These take-overs always are."

He threw her a final glance of contempt before turning on his heel and walking out of the place.

After Kurt had gone, Margaret remained quite still in the center of the room, staring through the open door, watching his powerful figure disappear from view. She was so shaken that she didn't hear approaching footsteps coming from the opposite direction, but a moment later another figure filled the aperture and with a start she realized that it was Bruce.

He looked at her for a long moment, then asked, "Who was that man?"

She pulled herself together and told him that it was Kurt Dahl, a local forester. Bruce immediately wanted to know why he had been visiting her chalet.

"He wanted to talk to me. Why not?" she spoke casually, picked up her handbag, and led the way outside.

Walking toward the hotel Bruce said rather complainingly that he had been looking for her all morning, adding that he had come to the chalet early on, only to find it empty.

"I went for a walk before breakfast," she told him.

"With that man?"

"By myself," she answered with a touch of impatience, and was glad when Bruce said no more. Indignant as she had been, she now felt in little mood to talk. Kurt had left her greatly disturbed, and she was troubled by the fact that he knew so much about Bruce. She was also troubled by the knowledge that Bruce not only owned extensive business concerns, but was a financier of international repute.

Disinclined as she was to talk, she could not let the matter rest. "There's something I'd like to discuss with you," she said.

"Then let's discuss it now. After that, I'm off to Bergen." He glanced at his watch. "It's only twelve, but we can have an early lunch."

She didn't tell him that she had had a very late breakfast, because she knew that he would ask why, so she let him lead her into the dining room.

Bruce ordered fjord trout with a strong

mustard sauce which was a speciality of the place, followed by wafer thin slices of *Spekeskinke*, the eggs spiced with chives. Again Margaret only toyed with the food, deliberately ignoring Bruce's glance of concern.

"What are you going to Bergen for?" she asked suddenly.

"To deal with things — the inquest, and establishing your father's death." He added, "I hope you won't be tempted to go climbing or anything reckless like that while I'm gone. You look tired. Why don't you rest?"

"I probably will. After that, I may take a walk — down to the fjord, perhaps, but maybe as far as the forests. Are you interested in forests?"

"I enjoy exploring them. But you know that. We have walked together in forests at home."

He smiled at her and she thought, as she always thought when with him, how kind his smile was. The sad thing about it was the emphasis it placed on his facial scar, deepening it into a line which looked sharp and painful.

She felt sorry for Bruce. He had been

a staunch friend to her father and to herself. She remembered how protective he had been at the time of her divorce, when she felt as if her life had cracked in two. Only then had he talked about his wife and son, and for the first time she had glimpsed what real sorrow was. When a reserved man let someone see his true feelings, the impact went deep, and she had known then that all Bruce's success had never obliterated the memory of his wife, or compensated for her loss. Work, for him, had become a stopgap, an escape, a seeking after forgetfulness.

All this passed through her mind now as she saw him looking at her with his usual gentleness, and suddenly she found it impossible to tell him about Kurt Dahl's accusations. The story of a take-over might be true, but the remaining facts just had to be wrong. Bruce was an honest man, totally reliable; not a man to go about things in a devious way.

And how could she set the word of someone whom she had known for barely a couple of days against her father's judgment of a man's character? Angus would never have gone into partnership with anyone unscrupulous.

But despite these arguments something compelled her to say, "You have business interests in Norway, haven't you, Bruce?"

"Paper mills in Bergen; others in Stavanger."

"So forests like these would be valuable to you?"

"Not to own. It costs less and is far less trouble to buy my wood-pulp direct from the mills. I buy in bulk from a firm with whom I've had a worthwhile contract for years." He added, "Why this sudden curiosity about my Norwegian holdings?" When she hesitated, he urged, "Tell me. You've something on your mind. I know you well, Margaret. You can't hide anything from me."

She told him then that she had heard that some financial concern was trying to take over the local forests, which would mean devastation and industrialization of the entire area.

He looked at her in astonishment, then broke into a laugh.

"You surely don't believe that *I* would have anything to do with such a scheme? Can you imagine me destroying such countryside as this? You know me better, Margaret. Any person who owned paper mills would be against the destruction of forests. That's logic."

She felt a touch of shame and he continued, "What, or who, put the idea into your head? This man Dahl? You said he was a forester. Did the story come from him?"

"About the take-over, yes."

"He can't imagine I'm tied up in a scheme like that? He doesn't even know me; we've never met. I hope he intends to fight?"

"Very definitely."

"Then good luck to him." Bruce dismissed the whole thing and went on to advise her not to roam too far away during his absence. "I'd like you to be here when I get back. And don't worry about a thing. I'll cope with it all; and tomorrow we can leave for home."

The mention of home brought into her mind the recollection of their business ties in Edinburgh and, even more sharply, the realization that now that her father had gone, she and Bruce would be sole partners. She would need his guidance and help, for hitherto all business matters had been handled by the two men. If Bruce showed the patience and concern which had been evident since the death of Angus, she would be grateful indeed. She looked at him with a smile, her heart warming to him. He wouldn't change. His solicitude and kindness would become a vital part of her life.

18

AS soon as Bruce had left for Bergen, Margaret set off to find the Church of St. Olaf. It was easy to trace for, as Brandt had told her, it stood in the center of the village, but apart from that its historic stave structure was eye-catching.

One main gate served both the church and the pastor's house adjoining. That too was built of wood, with jutting eaves and balconies.

Brandt opened the door himself. He showed no surprise, but commented ruefully, "I knew you were still in Voshanger. Your father would never heed advice, either."

He held the door wide and she stepped into a small hallway, from which led a rather cluttered sitting room. Brandt cleared a space for her to sit, sweeping a pile of papers onto the floor and dumping a discarded cup and saucer into the hearth. It was obvious that it didn't occur to him to apologize for the disorder because he was accustomed to it and therefore unaware of it. He was a man who would always be unaware of his surroundings.

Margaret came to the object of her visit.

"Why didn't you tell me about my father's house?"

Brandt looked surprised. "Didn't you know about it?"

"How could I? You know I have never been here before."

The man answered frankly, "To tell you the truth, I never gave it a thought. I had forgotten your father even owned a house here. He never visited it."

In surprise, Margaret asked why, and learned that Brandt had no idea, and that the house stood empty, deserted. A forgotten house, he called it.

"Then he must have owned it for a long time," Margaret commented.

"I believe he built it years ago."

"And never stayed in it?" Margaret was incredulous. "Then why didn't he sell?"

Brandt admitted he had asked that question himself on the only occasion when Angus had referred to the house. "Your father was a reserved man who rarely talked about himself or his past, but some time after we knew each other he mentioned that he had built the house before he met your mother."

As long ago as that, Margaret reflected in amazement . . . and he had never brought Nina back to Voshanger, even though he owned a house in the vicinity. The whole thing seemed not merely puzzling, but inexplicable.

She questioned Brandt about her father's explanation as to why he didn't sell, and learned that it had consisted only of a shrug.

"He was quite indifferent about the place," the man told her. "Not only did he keep away from it, but he neglected it. It is almost falling to ruin."

Margaret asked for the location of the house, more anxious than ever to see it. She felt it might reveal yet another unsuspected side of her father's character, another chapter in his life, hitherto unknown.

Brandt told her unwillingly that it was some distance outside the village,

259

situated at the base of remote foothills. But that wasn't enough. She wanted to know how to find it, adding that if he didn't tell her she would have to go back to Sonja Thorsen. The pastor looked surprised and Margaret told him, with some satisfaction, that she had learned of the house through the hotel manageress.

"And that was something else you kept from me," she added. "The story of Sonja Thorsen and my father."

Brandt pointed out that the only important thing, to him, had been the necessity for Margaret to leave Voshanger. That was why he had called to see her, and compared to that nothing else mattered.

"As for Sonja and Angus," he added, "I imagined you might have known, but if your father didn't tell you, why should I? Their affair concerned no one but themselves."

Margaret had no answer to that. She felt suddenly inadequate, rather foolish, coming to this man's house almost in a mood of accusation. Hans Brandt seemed an honest man with reasonable answers for everything.

She said helplessly, "Surely you must have realized that I would want to learn every possible thing about my father? His life here seems to have been separate and apart — I am discovering that more and more. And now, out of the blue, I hear he owned a house near Voshanger! I want to see it."

"There is nothing to prevent you, but I would advise against it."

"Why? Because you think I am being morbid?"

Margaret noticed that the man's eyes became slightly wary before he answered, "No. Because its locality is — lonely."

"Why should that put me off? Every climber is accustomed to solitude. If my father built his house in an isolated spot, I can understand it. Amongst the foothills, you say? I expect that was because it gave access to the mountains."

Brandt looked away. His evasiveness whetted Margaret's determination and she demanded to know exactly how to find the house. The man finally yielded and told her that it was on the way to the Cleft of Fenris.

A chill ran through her. She heard

261

herself saying, "Helga warned me to avoid that area too . . . "

Brandt asked on a quick note of surprise, "When did you meet Helga?"

Margaret told him about her visit with Kurt Dahl and of Helga's offer to supply climbing charts, marking danger spots and, in particular, the area of the cleft. "I also learned something which distressed and angered me, and I am sure you know what it was."

Brandt moved uncomfortably. "You mean the story of her accident?"

"Not the true story, merely that they both believe my father caused it. It was Sonja Thorsen who told me the truth this morning. She also gave me Helga's version. All this you kept from me."

Brandt spread his hands. "Why should I do otherwise? If you were already aware of it, you would have your own views. If you were unaware, it was better that you should remain so."

Margaret began to feel that she was up against an unyielding wall, and pointed out with some annoyance that he still had not told her exactly how to find her father's house. "I don't even know in which direction the Cleft of Fenris lies!"

A clock ticked somewhere in the silent room, and the sun penetrated through a window like a spotlight upon a stage. Margaret was aware of a million specks dancing along its shaft, but she was also aware of the sudden clash of this man's will against her own.

Finally he gave a reluctant sigh. "Very well," he said uneasily, "follow the fjord road toward the forests. Halfway there you will see a rocky projection upon a mountain slope. That is the buttress which hides the entrance to the Cleft of Fenris."

"How will I recognize it? The slopes have many rocky projections."

"But none quite like this. It is reminiscent of a wolf's head."

She thrust aside an impression of menace and asked with an effort, "And the house?"

"Just off the fjord road, beneath the shadow of the rock."

It didn't sound like an attractive situation for a house, but when she asked Brandt if he knew of any reason why her father chose such a site the man shook his head and went on to say that the place was partially hidden by trees and approached by an unpaved road — a slight hill, little more than a track.

She turned to the door at once, and as she did so Brandt urged her only to visit the house, and not to go on to the cleft. There were forces, he said, which she might unleash.

"Forces? What kind of forces? And how could I unleash them?"

"The same way that people can restart an avalanche after it appears to have settled — movement or sound can trigger it off again. That is why local police don't go near the cleft until some time after an eruption; it could flare up again, like a dormant volcano. I begged your father not to go back for that reason, but he refused to wait."

"Then how long was it before a search was made?"

"As I told you the other night — as soon as it was safe to go."

"Then it must be safe for me to go there now." She finished gently, "Don't worry. I've no intention of going near the

Cleft of Fenris, but nothing will stop me from visiting my father's house."

★ ★ ★

Walking along the winding fjord road, Margaret caught glimpses of the buttress which marked the entrance to the Cleft of Fenris long before she reached the foothills beneath it. The projection stood out like a landmark against the sky and, as Brandt had said, it was strangely reminiscent of a wolf, a gigantic creature which seemed to alternately beckon and then threaten. There was a sinister touch about it, but she kept it in sight as a guiding point until reaching the foothills below.

To her surprise the search for the track leading to the house proved to be difficult. By the time she discovered it — suddenly, accidentally, for it turned abruptly into the foothills and was almost obscured by trees — the sun was sliding westwards down the sky, chased by ominous clouds heralding an impending storm.

Anxiety touched her then, for if the light failed she would be unable to explore the house and the possibility of having to wait until tomorrow, evading Bruce and his determination to take her back to Scotland, sent her hurrying up the track in almost desperate haste.

Combined with this feeling of urgency she was conscious of excitement as the track rose in a gradual incline, ablaze with shrubs and alpine plants. Looking up, she saw the lowering sun between overhanging trees. Leaves spread like fans above her head, then suddenly the track widened and behind dense foliage stood the house. Log-hewn, rugged, handsome as a strong man marked with age.

She approached it slowly. Its setting was beautiful. If the screen of overgrown trees were cut back, the windows would command fine views of fjord and forest and mountain, and because the rear of the house was built close into the hillside, nothing could be seen of the sinister projection far above. Here was an isolated patch of time-worn beauty; a place which slept, forgotten.

Sadness took hold of her as she walked through the wilderness which had once been intended for a garden, and saw the crumbling woodwork and rotting steps of the house. The neglect all about her was tragic, and she felt a longing to put it right. Her father had had an affinity with this part of the world. Her mother's roots were here. Part of herself belonged to Voshanger and she felt a strange urge to identify herself with the place permanently.

As she climbed the front steps of the house, avoiding broken timbers, she noticed that curtains were drawn across the windows and that the door was fastened with a large wooden latch which appeared to be firmly embedded in its socket. To her surprise it lifted with ease. Also to her surprise, the door was unlocked and the hinges made no sound when she opened it.

She took a couple of steps inside, then pulled up sharply. She had expected darkness; instead, light blazed from candles at the far end of the room.

For a moment the flames appeared to hang in space, darkness above and below, and then she realized that the candles were black, standing upon a table shrouded in black, and that in the center of the table was a photograph, its frame draped in black. And the glass was smashed.

Standing poised in front of the picture, its point dug savagely into the table, was a dagger. Margaret took a step forward, and it quivered with vibrations from the bare wooden floor.

The atmosphere was macabre, but something compelled her to approach that table. She had to see the face behind the broken glass. With every step the dagger quivered, and the candle flame flickered, until it seemed that both were executing a dance of triumph. Then she stumbled to a halt.

Behind the broken glass she saw the face of her father.

She knew instinctively that this was an altar of hate. She had never seen such a thing before and the horror of it chilled her. Someone hated her father to such a degree that they had erected this dreadful thing against him.

She felt faint, and the candle flames seemed to advance and recede, backwards and forwards, mesmerizing her. She closed her eyes against them, and the world spun blackly. Then a sound penetrated her reeling sense — sharp, staccato, pulling her back to reality. The firm sound of approaching footsteps.

They were coming downstairs. They were coming this way. Margaret spun around, her eyes open and her nerves suddenly ice-cold and steady. She made no movement, waiting breathlessly until the owner of the footsteps came walking into the room.

It was Helga Carlsen.

19

SHOCK was violent, the truth unbelievable. There was no sign of a wheel chair.

This couldn't possibly be Helga, Margaret thought through stupefied senses. It had to be some other woman, one who held herself erect, walked briskly, moved with the ease of a person who had never been crippled. A woman with Helga's ravaged face wearing bizarre jewelery. A caricature of Helga, dressed in a long and vividly embroidered gown, with a headdress like that of a high priestess crowning smoothly coiled hair, and jewel-studded sandals covering strong and supple feet.

It was Helga as she might have appeared in some grossly theatrical drama; unreal, out of character, non-existent, except for the fact that she halted abruptly at the sight of Margaret and her eyes revealed not only astonishment but all the guilt and fear and evasion of someone trapped in a terrible secret.

Those were Helga's eyes without a doubt, their normal force and intelligence burning with double intensity, a fanatical intensity which told Margaret that this was no dream. She knew instinctively that she was face to face with the creature who had erected this diabolical altar and who paraded before the eyes of the world as a helpless cripple.

Margaret's glance flew to the picture of her father behind its savagely broken glass and a terrible anger surged through her.

"You hated him!" she gasped. "You hated him so much that you've lied and cheated all these years!"

"*And* got away with it," Helga declared proudly. She had quickly recovered from her initial shock and now her handsome face, grotesque with its mask of make-up, smiled triumphantly.

Margaret backed away, for about this woman was an aura of terrifying power. Even her voice seemed to hold a different timbre as she added, "I've fooled everyone — but all people are fools, easily duped."

"Except my father," Margaret cried.

The mask-like face became hard and contemptuous "*Including* your father. Even he believed my injuries were genuine, although he saved my life when he thrust me to safety. But what was my life without him? I watched him carried away on the second avalanche and prayed to God to see him killed."

Margaret gestured toward the altar of hate. "A woman like you doesn't believe in God. And how *dare* you erect that vile thing in my father's house?"

"Because it is *my* house," Helga answered blandly. "He gave it to me." She laughed at the disbelief in Margaret's face and continued, "It is true and I can prove it. He gave it to me to salve his conscience. As if I would be satisfied with a gesture like that! I had to pay him back for what he had done. And her. You know who I am talking about, don't you? Your mother."

Margaret fell silent. Fear, disbelief, a desire to escape and a desire to hear more, all vied within her, but dominant above everything was the sudden awareness that at last she was going to hear the truth about her mother's death. Haunted, Sonja had said. Doomed. By what, by whom?

I've got to know, Margaret insisted in her frightened mind. I've got to face it. I can't run away.

"What had my mother done to you?" she whispered. "She was gentle, sweet — "

"Sweet as sugar. Pretty as a picture," Helga sneered, "blonde like you, but without your strength. Oh, you have strength, Mrs. Drummond, I'll grant you that. I recognized it the moment I met you, even though you did startle me, walking in like that — as if you were Nina back from the dead. But Nina never had your character, or your will-power, or your endurance. Who gave you that? Who taught it to you? Not only your father, I'm sure. It takes emotional tempering to produce your kind of self-control."

As she spoke, Helga moved forward slowly. Her step was light, but firm; there was also a predatory quality about it, like an animal stalking its prey.

Margaret controlled a shudder and edged away, pretending to study the furnishings of the room although inwardly repelled by what she saw. All of it revealed a macabre taste, but rather than betray her reaction she went on examining the room, her ear attuned to that smooth and stealthy tread and the smooth and coaxing voice.

"Was it a man?" Helga persisted. "Did he make you suffer? Tell me about this man who hurt you. What was he? A waster? A sponger? Many men are only interested in women who have money. But Angus didn't love *me* because I had money. He loved me because I was young and beautiful and courageous, and could scale mountains with him and climb to the highest peaks."

The voice broke, then finished bitterly, "And then he met Nina. A stupid creature to my mind, but he rejected me for her."

"And never regretted it," Margaret taunted, unable to resist the opportunity to thrust the truth home, "but you have spent your life brooding over a rejection, a hurt to your pride!"

Helga flared, "Do *you* know what it feels like to be cast aside?"

"Yes — but it happened to me after I was married, not before, and that is worse. But do you think I am going to spend the rest of my life hating my husband because he fell in love with someone else?"

Helga whispered excitedly, "You should, you *must*. You can strike back — hurt him as he hurt you. Hurt them both."

"I don't want to." When the woman looked at her in surprise Margaret said impatiently, "Can't you understand? It's all in the past, and *I don't want to*. Hatred, vengeance — they would poison my mind as they have poisoned yours."

Helga drew herself up. "You shouldn't have said that. You've made a mistake, Mrs. Drummond. I am High Priestess of the Cult of Fenris. Take care that you don't insult me."

She was grotesque in her dignity, almost comic, but Margaret said angrily, "And what do you call this thing, this insult to my father, this crude and monstrous altar?"

Helga smiled and went across to it, touching the black draperies as if relishing the feel of them, then her voice echoed through the room again.

"I am proud of this altar. I used it to destroy him. I have been practicing against him for years, alone here without anyone knowing. There was a strength and resistance in him which was hard to overcome, but I won him in the end. He stayed away for a long time, loving his precious Nina and imagining he had made atonement to me by giving me this house."

Margaret burst out, "*Atonement*? What had he to atone for? Certainly not for injuring you — he saved your life! And in return you've acted out a wicked charade all these years."

Helga paid no heed. She seemed to be reliving the past, bringing it to life in front of Margaret's eyes, as if at last she had found an audience for which she had been starved.

"'Keep it,' he said, that last day we went climbing together. 'I was building it for you. I never wanted a house near that place. You chose the site, and you can keep it.' That is what he actually said."

The woman turned her painted face

to Margaret; it wore an expression of injured surprise.

"Would you believe that anyone could dislike such a spot as this? He admired the view — the fjord and forests and mountains beyond — but not that stretch above. Sinister, he called it! He even said once that he thought the cleft looked evil, but he loved me so much that he wanted me to choose where we would live. So I chose this place in order to be near the cleft."

Margaret realized that her expression must have betrayed her, for Helga said in astonishment that she wouldn't look like that if she knew what the cleft was like, and that even when young it had held a fascination for her. "As soon as I learned to climb I would go up there alone, and imagine the sabbats which used to be held there, and wish I could see them."

"But how did you learn when to stay away?" Margaret questioned, wondering how to lead the woman back to the subject of her mother and resolving not to leave this house until she had done so. She was now convinced that Helga knew the secret of Nina's death.

Helga told her that wise people had always known, adding boastfully that even as a child she used to listen to their talk, and ask questions, and store up the answers.

A strong lassitude seemed to be taking hold of Margaret, but through it she heard the sultry voice telling her how she had finally destroyed Angus Buchanan.

"I was in this house at the time, practicing against him. I heard the rumble high above. I love to be here when that happens, it excites me and I know I am safe because that overhanging buttress is a protection."

Margaret realized that her eyes were focused on the altar. Helga was standing beside it, glittering in the candlelight. It was impossible to turn her glance away; the voice of the priestess, the dancing flames, the flashing blade of the dagger, all mesmerized her.

She felt her eyelids begin to droop and fought to control them. From far away she heard Helga boasting that she never failed, that what she wanted to destroy, she destroyed.

Somehow Margaret managed to ask what she was seeking to destroy now, but her voice sounded remote even in her own ears.

"An enemy. Someone who seeks to abolish the cult. But he won't succeed."

Brandt, thought Margaret vaguely. So she knew about Brandt and his aims . . .

From beneath heavy eyelids Margaret saw the High Priestess smile. There was relish in the curve of the painted mouth, satisfaction in the burning eyes as she went on to relate how for years she had willed Angus to return to Voshanger and that when he did, she came to this house to work against him in secret.

"I wanted to destroy him *here*. That was vitally important to me. But he had that strange power of resistance, constantly balking me — "

With an effort Margaret pointed out that her father had possessed moral resistance. "A hatred of evil of everything you believed in — your cult and its practices."

Helga said sharply, "Our practices? Only the initiated know them."

With an even greater effort, Margaret

turned her back upon the black table with its mesmeric lights. She moved at the precise moment that Helga came and stood before her, so close that Margaret could smell the exotic perfume she wore. That, too, had a hypnotic effect and she moved further away, leaving the light shining full on the woman's face.

Now Helga was saying urgently, "I like you, Margaret Drummond, despite your parents. You are intelligent, and have courage. You are sensitive too, beneath that outer display of calm. You feel deeply. You would be good material. Put yourself in my hands and I can reveal secrets you never dreamed of; power unlimited. You think you know the practices of the cult? All you can possibly know is the ridiculous nonsense published in books on witchcraft or shown in horror films."

"I know that Fenris was the son of Loki and Augurboda," Margaret said, watching the woman's face and seeing the mouth curve derisively.

"I told you that when Kurt brought you to see me, Mrs. Drummond. Poor Kurt, he hasn't the slightest suspicion of the truth. Like everyone else, he thinks I am a helpless cripple. Even members of the cult believe it. I have to be carried up the mountainside whenever the group meets, although I could climb it with ease — and often do, from this house, when I know it is safe and that no one is likely to be around. This house is my refuge. I can do what I like here without risk."

Margaret refused to believe that someone could pretend to be a helpless cripple for so many years, and get away with it, but Helga assured her that it had been done many times and that history was full of clever people like herself. Besides, it had been an essential part of her punishment of Angus Buchanan, a permanent reproach, a reminder that he had ruined her life.

"I wanted the world to believe it too, and the world did!"

"And — all this?" Margaret asked, "When did you become interested in this?" She indicated the trappings of Black Magic around the room.

"I've always been interested," Helga admitted, "but when Angus fell in love with Nina, I began to study in earnest. I ordered books, the right books, by mail from Oslo, from London, even as far as New York. I built up a library — it is stored in this house."

She certainly had a good hide-out here, Margaret thought, well screened from the road and off the beaten track. And it would be easy enough to drive an invalid-car up that rough little incline and hide it close to the house. Everyone believed the place to be shut up and empty, and the illusion was well preserved.

She heard Helga saying, "I couldn't have a better sanctuary than this. Only initiated members of the cult ever take this track leading up to the cleft, and they only come for the sabbats. We meet outside and they carry me up the mountainside. I initiated every one of them, all who I sensed were good material, the right material for a cult of this kind. And once initiated, there is no going back, no chance to desert. To reveal its existence means death."

Her hand whipped out and snatched up the dagger. The flash of its blade was repeated in the flash of her eyes.

There was a maniacal look about her which made Margaret turn cold.

"So you see, don't you, Mrs. Drummond, that because you have come here and discovered my secret and learned so much, I can't let you leave this house? You do understand that, don't you, my dear?"

Her voice had the smoothness of silk and her step was strangely silent as she came closer. Margaret edged away. Fear had the cold sensation of steel but somehow she managed to speak.

"Killing me won't help you. My father managed to get evidence, undeniable evidence. Photographs of your rites."

"You're lying! Angus Buchanan knew nothing about the cult and he disliked that cleft so much that he would never go near it. And if the uninitiated ever stumbled upon a sabbat, they would never escape."

"But *he* did. He hid himself and used a specialized film which required neither flash bulbs nor infra-red. I have the negatives."

Helga laughed aloud. "You're bluffing. No one can outwit me."

"But my father did," Margaret insisted, still edging away.

The dagger followed relentlessly as Helga went on to declare that she had achieved final vengeance by using will-power to compel him to visit the mountainside and so meet his death.

"You are wrong," Margaret declared. "It was through me that he came. He always carried my picture with him, and the night he photographed your hideous rites he dropped it somewhere, and then went back for it. His death was accidental, but perhaps he would have been protected had he worn the Varuna ring."

For the first time, Helga seemed touched by alarm, demanding to hear what Margaret knew about Varuna.

"That he is the all-seeing one, the enemy of Fenris and all the legendary gods of evil."

Helga lifted her head defiantly and declared that one day she would be greater than Varuna. "More powerful than I am now — and my power is already great. Shall I tell you how great?"

The woman paused, then continued

with relish, "My first victory was with your mother. I killed her. Slowly. Inch by inch and minute by minute. I did it with the power of my mind. She was to waste away . . . gradually . . . and that is how she died. It took me a long time, but I enjoyed every moment. The longer she suffered, the longer Angus suffered too. Every minute, every second was one of revenge and I delighted in them . . . "

It was then that Margaret's self-control finally broke and outrage took over. She dived for the altar, seized a candlestick and hurled it in the woman's face. It struck the side of her head and beneath the sound of her scream Margaret heard the dagger clatter to the floor.

With one wide sweep she sent the remaining candles scattering and saw the drapes catch fire. Racing for the door, she could hear the crackling of dry wood as flames licked the floor.

She was out of the house and running across the wild garden with Helga stumbling after her when she pitched headlong into Kurt Dahl. He caught and held her, but she thrust him aside.

"*Helga — get her!*"

There was just enough light to see a rough path ahead. Margaret took it automatically, her only desire being to get away from that house. After a few minutes she realized that she had missed the track leading down to the road, but the path was level and must surely descend.

She stumbled on, and suddenly the night was black, with thunder rumbling ominously beyond the mountains. Then the deluge came and she began to grope helplessly for shelter, her hands and feet meeting nothing but rock and loose stones. Somehow she would have to retrace her steps, but in the darkness she had lost all sense of direction.

After a while she realized that instead of descending she was climbing. She looked around blindly, seeking a way back, and at that moment a jagged fork of lightning sliced the sky ahead, outlining the massive dominating buttress — a gigantic rock shaped uncannily like a wolf.

She was heading straight for the Cleft of Fenris.

20

THERE was no going back, for below was only darkness, and even as Margaret stood hesitating her foot slipped on the rough earth, sending a shower of loose stones catapulting into space. She heard them ricochet against the walls of an unseen crevasse which she had miraculously avoided in her hasty ascent. One false step downward, and she would go after them.

Faced with the choice of remaining where she was, exposed to the storm, or of seeking shelter at a higher level, her common sense urged her forward. Somewhere beneath that overhanging ridge there must be some protected spot in which she could hide.

She went forward carefully, waiting for intermittent lightning to aid her, and seeing, in these intervals, a steep ascent leading toward the buttress. Thunder reverberated across the mountainside, hurling itself against the immovable wall of rock then retreating with a roar like frustrated rage.

Margaret's clothes felt damp; wet hair streamed over her shoulders. She pushed it back impatiently as she staggered onward and upward, no longer heeding the sinister appearance of the projecting rock, aware only that its vast bulk offered protection.

Lightning became more constant, an almost continuous illumination revealing the wild landscape above and around her, and as she approached the cleft she was staggered by the immensity of its protective buttress. From the valley it appeared to be no more than a huge out-thrust from the mountainside, but at close quarters it was more like a barricading wall protecting the approach to a city.

She knew now why Helga had been unafraid, down there in her house of hatred, when Fenris raged behind this bastion.

Somewhere within its span was the entrance to the cleft. Margaret had no desire to penetrate so far, but only to find shelter beneath the overhang, and as she paused to seek a likely spot there came a lull in the storm; lightning died and thunder was silenced. Even the rain lost its sullen roar and became no more than a whisper of sound, so that beneath it other sounds penetrated — sliding stones, the crunch of loose gravel, the measured tread of a heavy stride following in her wake . . .

She peered into the surrounding gloom, but could see nothing. Thrusting down a feeling of alarm, she pressed on, but as she climbed higher and higher she had the uncanny feeling that she was being followed. Fear quickened her steps and to calm herself she recalled that at such a height as this it was easy to mistake the echo of her own footsteps for those of others.

The storm came rumbling back, roaring like angry gods mustering for attack, with lightning as their fiery vanguard. Margaret halted for breath, and looked up. Above and beyond the ridge of Fenris, the towering peak of the mountain disappeared into blackened skies dwarfing the immense projection and reducing her to the ignominy of an ant on the surface of the lower earth. Yet even this level felt like some remote and uncharted world, desolate, sinister, filled with spirits from the past.

She was about to press forward again when she became convinced that her feeling of being followed was not imaginary. She could hear footsteps coming closer, heavy and determined.

Lightning revealed a nearby screen of rock and scrub. She moved swiftly and crouched behind it. The moment she was hidden, renewed lightning threw the world into startling relief and suddenly a shape materialized out of the vividly illuminated scene.

For a moment, she was transfixed. Every vein in her body seemed to freeze. The figure coming up the slope behind her carried a climber's powerful torch. Then Margaret recognized him and tremendous thankfulness welled up, sending her stumbling from her hiding-place.

"Bruce! *Bruce!*"

She was almost sobbing as he reached out and grasped her. She clung to him, hearing him say that he had come to find her because he had a hunch she might be up here.

"God knows why, but I didn't believe you when you promised to rest — something made me race back from Bergen. I got here as fast as I could."

He helped her into the shadow of the overhang; descent would be difficult until the storm eased, and it soon became apparent that instead of sheltering them the overhanging rock formed a trap, the rain beating in at almost gale force.

Above the din he shouted to her to hold on to him, and began to inch his way along the rock face, scanning the surface with the beam from his torch, looking for some crevice deep enough to shelter them. Then suddenly he gave a shout and pulled her after him. They were in a gap just wide enough for them to walk through in single file, and it led straight into the cleft.

Instinctively, she held back, but he urged her on. The reverse side would be the sheltered side, he pointed out. She saw the logic of that and made no further protest, but once within the cleft they both stood still. The torch-beam spanned an area blackened and desolate, a devastated gorge surrounded by barren walls.

Margaret shuddered and Bruce said, "Horrible, isn't it? I've heard of this place, but never imagined anything like this. Let's see if there isn't some shelter — "

Slowly, he moved the torch in a wide arc. Its light traveled across bleak earth and bare rock surfaces where no vegetation survived, then suddenly he held it still, spotlighting the entrance to a cave. With a satisfied exclamation, he took hold of her hand and hurried her forward.

Once through the darkly yawning entrance of the cave, Margaret began to shiver violently. Her clothes were now drenched and coldness seeped through her. Bruce led her further into the cave, the torch revealing that it was really a tunnel leading to a deeper opening beyond.

Margaret was grateful because his protective concern was not tinged with reproof, even though she had landed them in this predicament through her own folly.

His presence was reassuring, also his smile as he looked down at her.

She heard him say, "This is better — you'll be warmer in here," and she saw then that the tunnel had opened out into a cavern.

Now she was aware of nothing but mounting horror as the unforgettable photograph leaped to life before her eyes. She realized that they were standing in the very place where it had been taken.

Blindly she turned to run — only to come up against a barrier.

It was Bruce's arm.

He said gently, "There is no need to be alarmed. You are safe here — with me."

Over his shoulder she saw the whole width of the cavern spreading out before her, with the same shadowy background as in the photograph. Angus had focused on the main drama, but now she saw something which had been only faintly discernible in the picture — a throne on which had sat a robed figure, shadowy and unrecognizable, but which Margaret now realized had been the High Priestess, Helga herself — and there, in the middle of the cavern, was the place where the central figure had been poised in action as her father obtained his damning evidence against him.

She whispered, "You don't understand, Bruce. This place is evil!"

"And how do you know that? Was it — in the film?"

Her whole body went numb, and it seemed as if the walls of the cavern came rushing toward her and that Bruce's face was doing the same thing — swaying backward and forward, as the candle flames had swayed on Helga's altar of hate. But all the time he smiled with the same concern, the same kindness, but now the scar on his face showed up like a livid weal.

When her senses steadied a little, Margaret asked, "How do you know about the film?"

"You told me about it. And you did process it."

She remembered then. She had told him during lunch at the Roxburghe, but he had not believed her; he had dismissed her story as if it were something she had imagined.

She drew away from him, conscious of an underlying uncertainty. He let her go.

"Mrs. McFee told me of your phone call, saying you intended to go around — and I was there anyway, in the secret passage."

She gasped, "You were spying on me!"

"I had rung your flat and got no reply. I was curious about that film so I went along to your father's house to see if you had taken it there. I've always had a key. I was in the lab when I heard you arrive."

Margaret remembered her telephone ringing as she left the flat, and her car stalling until the battery was recharged. In that time Bruce had been able to reach the house in St. John's Street before her, and to hide himself as she worked. She also remembered something else — something more recent. His confident approach up the mountainside, his apparent familiarity with the track, his instinctive turn in the right direction to find the entrance to the cleft . . .

"You brought me here — you knew

the way! *You belong to the cult — "*

"If I could have laid my hands on that film, you would never have found out." His face was an implacable mask.

She spun away from him, but his hand shot out and caught her wrist.

"I could only attend the sabbats when I was in Norway, and this time I intended to put an end to it, to destroy the whole thing." There was a pleading note in his voice.

"So it was you Helga meant, not Brandt!"

"Before I return to Edinburgh, every trace will be destroyed. I mean to establish an industry here. I have local backing, everyone's confidence. To remain involved with the cult would ruin me."

"So you *are* behind the take-over! You lied to me — "

"I had to, for the time being."

"But my father knew nothing about it?"

He shook his head. "This was *my* project."

She retreated from him, but he continued urgently, "Don't you realize that we are on our own now? Your father is dead; the verdict at the inquest was death by misadventure. You inherit. Between us, we will own everything. But we can be more than partners." His voice was thick. "I have wanted you — "

"NO!"

The tunnel was only a few yards away and she had reached it by the time he seized her. She saw his eyes above her, full of longing.

"I don't want to hurt you, Margaret. Go along with me, and I'll look after you always." His tone hardened. "But betray me and — "

"I *will* betray you. I will *expose* you — "

Her words lashed him. With one violent movement she jerked free and went racing along the tunnel. She heard him close behind, shouting angrily. There was no gentleness in him now — only murderous violence.

A moment later his hands were upon her, terrifying in their strength. She was struggling, clawing, fighting for her life. She turned her head and bit deep into his wrist and his grip relaxed, accompanied by a cry of rage which was immediately drowned by a deafening crash of thunder.

She saw the jagged exit lit by lightning and raced for it. The air outside met her with a welcoming rush, and at that precise moment a second crash of thunder seemed to split the world apart. There was a deafening explosion behind her as the tunnel caved in, and the force of the blast threw her bodily into the outside world.

She lay stunned, vaguely aware of running footsteps, knowing that they belonged to Bruce and that she was powerless against him now.

She was dragged to her feet and held there. She stood rocking, obeying only half consciously when Kurt's voice urged her to lean on him and hurry — *hurry* . . . !

He half carried her, half dragged her, over the rough ground. They were choked by clouds of dust and pelted by flying stones, but gradually the roar behind them receded and they were stumbling through the aperture leading from the cleft to the mountainside.

★ ★ ★

She sat in Sonja Thorsen's sitting room, wrapped in a robe, a hot drink in hand. Kurt was there. He had brought her straight to the hotel and was now telling her how he had gone to Brandt, who told him everything, including her intention to visit Angus Buchanan's house, and that after the shock of seeing Helga running shakily, but obviously uncrippled, to her car and driving off at a dangerous and erratic speed, he had searched frantically for Margaret. Continuous lightning had revealed Matheson far up the slope, climbing purposefully toward the cleft, and had brought Kurt to her finally.

Bruce had been killed instantly; his body would lie forever in the sealed tunnel of the cavern.

The telephone rang. Kurt broke off to answer it and Margaret watched him as he talked, wondering how she could ever have mistrusted or feared him.

Then her thoughts came back to herself; she would have to return to Edinburgh because there were things to be dealt with, lawyers to see, all the red tape of winding things up. But after? She would come back. This man would bring her. They both knew it.

Kurt turned to her. "It's Brandt. He has news and wants me to pass it on to you."

The news was that Helga had been rushed to the hospital. Her car had crashed against some rocks beside the fjord road. There seemed to be no reason for the accident, but examination revealed that there were were no previous injuries; only those due to the crash.

"If she lives," Kurt finished, "she really will be crippled this time."

He held out the phone and Margaret heard Brandt's quiet, remote voice saying in her ear, " . . . and Mrs. Drummond is out of danger. Tell her I will let my brother know right away."

Margaret smiled. Naturally, she thought. The guru would be waiting.

TO FIGHT THE WILD
Rod Ansell and Rachel Percy

Lost in uncharted Australian bush, Rod Ansell survived by hunting and trapping wild animals, improvising shelter and using all the bushman's skills he knew.

COROMANDEL
Pat Barr

India in the 1830s is a hot, uncomfortable place, where the East India Company still rules. Amelia and her new husband find themselves caught up in the animosities which seethe between the old order and the new.

THE SMALL PARTY
Lillian Beckwith

A frightening journey to safety begins for Ruth and her small party as their island is caught up in the dangers of armed insurrection.

CLOUD OVER MALVERTON
Nancy Buckingham

Dulcie soon realises that something is seriously wrong at Malverton, and when violence strikes she is horrified to find herself under suspicion of murder.

AFTER THOUGHTS
Max Bygraves

The Cockney entertainer tells stories of his East End childhood, of his RAF days, and his post-war showbusiness successes and friendships with fellow comedians.

MOONLIGHT
AND MARCH ROSES
D. Y. Cameron

Lynn's search to trace a missing girl takes her to Spain, where she meets Clive Hendon. While untangling the situation, she untangles her emotions and decides on her own future.

NURSE ALICE IN LOVE
Theresa Charles

Accepting the post of nurse to little Fernie Sherrod, Alice Everton could not guess at the romance, suspense and danger which lay ahead at the Sherrod's isolated estate.

POIROT INVESTIGATES
Agatha Christie

Two things bind these eleven stories together — the brilliance and uncanny skill of the diminutive Belgian detective, and the stupidity of his Watson-like partner, Captain Hastings.

LET LOOSE THE TIGERS
Josephine Cox

Queenie promised to find the long-lost son of the frail, elderly murderess, Hannah Jason. But her enquiries threatened to unlock the cage where crucial secrets had long been held captive.

THE TWILIGHT MAN
Frank Gruber

Jim Rand lives alone in the California desert awaiting death. Into his hermit existence comes a teenage girl who blows both his past and his brief future wide open.

DOG IN THE DARK
Gerald Hammond

Jim Cunningham breeds and trains gun dogs, and his antagonism towards the devotees of show spaniels earns him many enemies. So when one of them is found murdered, the police are on his doorstep within hours.

THE RED KNIGHT
Geoffrey Moxon

When he finds himself a pawn on the chessboard of international espionage with his family in constant danger, Guy Trent becomes embroiled in moves and countermoves which may mean life or death for Western scientists.

TIGER TIGER
Frank Ryan

A young man involved in drugs is found murdered. This is the first event which will draw Detective Inspector Sandy Woodings into a whirlpool of murder and deceit.

CAROLINE MINUSCULE
Andrew Taylor

Caroline Minuscule, a medieval script, is the first clue to the whereabouts of a cache of diamonds. The search becomes a deadly kind of fairy story in which several murders have an other-worldly quality.

LONG CHAIN OF DEATH
Sarah Wolf

During the Second World War four American teenagers from the same town join the Army together. Forty-two years later, the son of one of the soldiers realises that someone is systematically wiping out the families of the four men.

THE LISTERDALE MYSTERY
Agatha Christie

Twelve short stories ranging from the light-hearted to the macabre, diverse mysteries ingeniously and plausibly contrived and convincingly unravelled.

TO BE LOVED
Lynne Collins

Andrew married the woman he had always loved despite the knowledge that Sarah married him for reasons of her own. So much heartache could have been avoided if only he had known how vital it was to be loved.

ACCUSED NURSE
Jane Converse

Paula found herself accused of a crime which could cost her her job, her nurse's reputation, and even the man she loved, unless the truth came to light.

A GREAT DELIVERANCE
Elizabeth George

Into the web of old houses and secrets of Keldale Valley comes Scotland Yard Inspector Thomas Lynley and his assistant to solve a particularly savage murder.

'E' IS FOR EVIDENCE
Sue Grafton

Kinsey Millhone was bogged down on a warehouse fire claim. It came as something of a shock when she was accused of being on the take. She'd been set up. Now she had a new client — herself.

A FAMILY OUTING IN AFRICA
Charles Hampton and Janie Hampton

A tale of a young family's journey through Central Africa by bus, train, river boat, lorry, wooden bicycle and foot.

THE PLEASURES OF AGE
Robert Morley

The author, British stage and screen star, now eighty, is enjoying the pleasures of age. He has drawn on his experiences to write this witty, entertaining and informative book.

THE VINEGAR SEED
Maureen Peters

The first book in a trilogy which follows the exploits of two sisters who leave Ireland in 1861 to seek their fortune in England.

A VERY PAROCHIAL MURDER
John Wainwright

A mugging in the genteel seaside town turned to murder when the victim died. Then the body of a young tearaway is washed ashore and Detective Inspector Lyle is determined that a second killing will not go unpunished.

DEATH ON A HOT SUMMER NIGHT
Anne Infante

Micky Douglas is either accident-prone or someone is trying to kill him. He finds himself caught in a desperate race to save his ex-wife and others from a ruthless gang.

HOLD DOWN A SHADOW
Geoffrey Jenkins

Maluti Rider, with the help of four of the world's most wanted men, is determined to destroy the Katse Dam and release a killer flood.

THAT NICE MISS SMITH
Nigel Morland

A reconstruction and reassessment of the trial in 1857 of Madeleine Smith, who was acquitted by a verdict of Not Proven of poisoning her lover, Emile L'Angelier.

SEASONS OF MY LIFE
Hannah Hauxwell
and Barry Cockcroft

The story of Hannah Hauxwell's struggle to survive on a desolate farm in the Yorkshire Dales with little money, no electricity and no running water.

TAKING OVER
Shirley Lowe and Angela Ince

A witty insight into what happens when women take over in the boardroom and their husbands take over chores, children and chickenpox.

AFTER MIDNIGHT STORIES,
The Fourth Book Of

A collection of sixteen of the best of today's ghost stories, all different in style and approach but all combining to give the reader that special midnight shiver.

DEATH TRAIN
Robert Byrne

The tale of a freight train out of control and leaking a paralytic nerve gas that turns America's West into a scene of chemical catastrophe in which whole towns are rendered helpless.

THE ADVENTURE
OF THE
CHRISTMAS PUDDING
Agatha Christie

In the introduction to this short story collection the author wrote "This book of Christmas fare may be described as 'The Chef's Selection'. I am the Chef!"

RETURN TO BALANDRA
Grace Driver

Returning to her Caribbean island home, Suzanne looks forward to being with her parents again, but most of all she longs to see Wim van Branden, a coffee planter she has known all her life.

SKINWALKERS
Tony Hillerman

The peace of the land between the sacred mountains is shattered by three murders. Is a 'skinwalker', one who has rejected the harmony of the Navajo way, the murderer?

A PARTICULAR PLACE
Mary Hocking

How is Michael Hoath, newly arrived vicar of St. Hilary's, to meet the demands of his flock and his strained marriage? Further complications follow when he falls hopelessly in love with a married parishioner.

A MATTER OF MISCHIEF
Evelyn Hood

A saga of the weaving folk in 18th century Scotland. Physician Gavin Knox was desperately seeking a cure for the pox that ravaged the slums of Glasgow and Paisley, but his adored wife, Margaret, stood in the way.

DEAD SPIT
Janet Edmonds

Government vet Linus Rintoul attempts to solve a mystery which plunges him into the esoteric world of pedigree dogs, murder and terrorism, and Crufts Dog Show proves to be far more exciting than he had bargained for . . .

A BARROW IN THE BROADWAY
Pamela Evans

Adopted by the Gordillo family, Rosie Goodson watched their business grow from a street barrow to a chain of supermarkets. But passion, bitterness and her unhappy marriage aliented her from them.

THE GOLD AND THE DROSS
Eleanor Farnes

Lorna found it hard to make ends meet for herself and her mother and then by chance she met two men — one a famous author and one a rich banker. But could she really expect to be happy with either man?

THE SONG OF THE PINES
Christina Green

Taken to a Greek island as substitute for David Nicholas's secretary, Annie quickly falls prey to the island's charms and to the charms of both Marcus, the Greek, and David himself.

GOODBYE DOCTOR GARLAND
Marjorie Harte

The story of a woman doctor who gave too much to her profession and almost lost her personal happiness.

DIGBY
Pamela Hill

Welcomed at courts throughout Europe, Kenelm Digby was the particular favourite of the Queen of France, who wanted him to be her lover, but the beautiful Venetia was the mainspring of his life.